A WRITER

ON

THE ROCKS

DOUG MCPHILLIPS

Other Visionary Stories

Novels

From Darkness to Light.
The Sword of Discernment.
Santiago Traveller.
I, Prophet.
Awake to my Gutted Dream.
We is Me Upside Down.
The Guru of Jerusalem
Masters at my table.
The Wicklow Way.
The Adventures of Ace McDice,
Stretch Deed & Moonshine Melody.
Instant karma and grace.
Reflections of an Old Man.
The Credo.
King of the O' Malley.
The One.

Albums
Country Camino
Santiago Traveller.
Soul Fact.

Doug McPhillips 2023
ISBN 978-064-58862-4-5

National Library of Australia Catalog-in-publication data: Damon
Runyon Omnibus, Amazon Books, 1940 Reprint.
We is me Upside Down, Doug McPhillips, Ingram Spark, 2021.

Contents. 3.

Introduction.5.

Chapter 1.   Facts about The Rocks.7.

Chapter 2.   Razor Gangs and Prostitutes.15.

Chapter 3.   The Downtown Push. 23.

Chapter 4.   Working the Alcoholic Mind. 37.

Chapter 5.   Living the life of Riley. 51.

Chapter 6.   How to run a profitable business. 63.

Chapter 7.   Burnt out Gizzard. 77.

Chapter 8.   Out on the Tiles. 89.

Chapter 9.   Hero of Inequity. 101.

Chapter 10. Crazy Capers in Cars. 113.

Chapter 11. Running to Stand Still 125.

Chapter 12.   The Last Hurrah 137.

Chapter 13. Senses and Sensibility. 149

For my old friends of The Push
Somehow out there
Somewhere,
Somewhat lost.

Introduction.

In the fellowship of Alcoholics Anonymous, a newcomer to the sobriety programme is encouraged to share the story of their drinking career, what happened, what changed and what it is like now.

This book is a collection of stories from the author's memory of former 'devil-may-care' days of his wild and wayward youth before he gave up the booze. He recounts the many characters he met during his drinking days and the trouble they and he caused in their efforts to enjoy life to the fullest. The plot is centred in and around the bars of the central business district of Sydney known as The Rocks. The writer describes his early drinking career as a prelude to entering the haunts centred around The Rocks during the 1960s. It is written focusing on the humorous side of his escapades whilst mainly under the weather from the effect of alcohol. There is a note of warning, however, for the not-so-faint-hearted to steer clear of having too much of a good thing at the expense of health, wealth and happiness. The writer could quickly tell of the tragic side of the ultimate outcomes of excessive drinking, but this novel focuses on the funny side of it all before the wake-up call to live a sober life dawned upon a tarried mind. Now read on...

Memorable quotes of my former like-minded drinkers that were true to my life at the time.

"Well, you see, Norm, it's like this. A herd of buffalo can only move as fast as the slowest buffalo. And when the herd is hunted, the slowest and weakest ones at the back are killed first. This natural selection is good for the herd because the general speed and health of the whole group keep improving through the regular killing of the weakest members. Similarly, the human brain can only operate as fast as the slowest brain cells. Excessive intake of alcohol, as we know, kills brain cells. But naturally, it attacks the slowest and weakest brain cells first. In this way, regular beer consumption eliminates the weaker brain cells, making the brain a faster and more efficient machine! That's why you always feel smarter after a few beers."

"Alcohol is not the answer; it just makes you forget the question."

"Alcohol is a perfect solvent; it dissolves marriages, families and careers."

"Alcohol doesn't affect me, affect me, affect me."

"They just don't make enough alcohol."

CHAPTER 1.

FACTS ABOUT THE ROCKS

The Rocks, to my wayward drinking nature of the decades of the 1960s, was my most frequented pub crawl location. So before delving into the stories that surrounded my life of scoffing down copious quantities of beer, rye whisky and excessive intake of cigarettes in the company of pseudo-intellectuals and loose women, it is only fair to tell of the history of the place that held for me so much fascination in those days of misspent youth. The Rocks is a small district near the heart of Sydney on the hillside above the western shore of Sydney Cove and Circular Quay. Here, Sydney's first permanent dwellings were built, a cluster of humble wattle and daub huts perched precariously amid the rocky inclines that gave the location its name.

The Rocks became established shortly after the colony's formation in 1788 as an initial prisoner location for convicts who arrived with the first fleet a year earlier. They were transported by ship from England mainly for petty crimes ranging from Grand Larceny, being theft above one shilling; Petty Larceny for theft below one shilling; receiving stolen goods or stealing lead, iron or copper, or being in the trade of buying or receiving these commodities. Some were transported for impersonating Egyptians, and others for stealing a loaf of bread. Thousands of miles from home, England's banished thieves were locked in a prison with ocean walls, forced to find food and cut through stone. Defying the odds, their shanty camp survived and grew—clutching to life on the banks of a freshwater stream. Gardens were grown, goods were traded & and rum soon ranked as both currency & and cure. As time passed, The Rocks were carved into cottages and corridors. Scallywags sailed into shore. Larrikins lurked in the laneways & and many a clever convict swapped their chains for riches. But While the governor and civil personnel lived on the more orderly eastern slopes of the Tank Stream, convict women and men appropriated land on the west.

They fenced off gardens and yards, established trades and businesses, built bread ovens and forges, opened shops and pubs, and raised families. They took in lodgers – the newly arrived convicts who slept in kitchens and skillions. Some emancipists also had convict servants. And there was always a pub for every four residential dwellings.

Most of the pub names recall lords, politicians and royalty of the British aristocracy of the early 19th century, the era in which The Rocks was being developed.   One of the colony's earliest streets, Brown Bear Lane, was close to where The Rocks' first pub, The Romping Horse, was on the corner of a lane from 1789. The pub was later known as The Brown Bear (1836–1900), while further up the lane was another hotel known as The Black Dog 1804–1848). Brown Bear Lane became Little Essex Street in the 1890s. The lane disappeared around 1913 when a row of shops was built between Essex Street and this location. Back in 1864, lodgings for visiting sailors arose as an alternative to the seedy inns and brothels that proliferated the Rocks, but this was just cover for the sailors of the military to be close to the action of the drinking life; prostitutes, gangsters and gaming that proliferated the streets and back allies of The Rocks back then.

Orderly, grid-patterned streets were impossible on the rugged terrain of The Rocks, and people moved about mainly on foot, so a web of footpaths led along and up the shelving ledges and from door to door. They soon had a stone church, St Philip's, at the southern periphery on Church Hill (now Lang Park), and several windmills creaked on the western horizon above. The walled jail and the town's first hospital stood at the foot of The Rocks in what later became George Street. Public and private wharves were clustered at the water's edge opposite, and the storehouses and elegant mansions of the early Sydney traders, fast-growing rich in the developing port town.

Surrounded by water on three sides, The Rocks was associated with seafaring, waterside workers and the maritime trades for most of its history. It was the link with the broader world, a place of new ideas, things and people. sailors from all over the world on shore leave and with the constant movement of people and goods through the port. While Governor Macquarie had straightened the other streets of Sydney during the 1810s, those of The Rocks remained crooked and uneven. It also remained a convicts' place, for when the men from Hyde Park Barracks (opened in 1819) were allowed out on Sundays after church 'they ran immediately to that part of the town they call the Rocks, where every species of Debauchery and villainy was practised'.

By 1823, about 1,200 people lived in The Rocks, most emancipists, convicts, and their children. The expansion and consolidation of trademarked the 1820s and 1830s, as merchants' and ship-owners houses, stores and wharves expanded right around Dawes Point to Millers Point and Cockle Bay (now Darling Harbour). A substantial stone bond store, built in 1826 on Argyle Street, served as the first Customs House and still stands as part of the Argyle Stores. The buildings on the surrounding slopes ranged from substantial two-storey residences, shops and hotels to small rental tenements of one or two rooms. Nearby, massive quarries around Observatory Hill supplied stone for building and left behind sheer cliff faces. The first housing subdivision began developing on the northern ends around Bunkers Hill. On the heights of Cumberland and Princes streets, wealthy middle-class people built elegant, fashionable mansions and townhouses.

After the end of transportation in 1840 and the discovery of gold in 1851, immigration to the colony rose dramatically, resulting in an intense demand for housing. The Rocks became where immigrants found their first foothold, squeezed into existing houses, and even converted stables.

Although piecemeal street-making, paving and drainage works were carried out constantly from the 1850s, progress has been slow, and the results quickly worn down or blocked up. Sewer lines were installed down the main streets in the 1850s, but only some houses were connected. Many houses had stone cesspits, and some had nothing at all. However, labour and funding could be found for works that assisted private enterprises. In 1843, convict gangs were put to work on a cut right through the ridge at the heart of The Rocks, extending Argyle Street to connect Sydney Cove with the booming area of Darling Harbour. Earlier, drays and people had to take the long way around, north or south. The rubble stone from the Argyle Cut was carted away to build an even larger project: the first stage of Circular Quay. But work was slow, and when the convict labour force dwindled, the Argyle Cut project stopped. It was eventually completed, using paid labour and gunpowder, in 1859. Bridges reconnected the severed streets above in the 1860s.

The area had been home to people of widely divergent classes over the nineteenth century – from the rich in their impressive houses on the ridges, ship captains and shopkeepers, to labourers and the drifting poor. But after the 1870s, this profile began to change as the wealthy increasingly abandoned city neighbourhoods for homes in the new suburbs.

The Rocks became an increasingly working-class area. It was also a place of fearful fascination for outsiders – it was always Sydney's 'other' place. Its proximity and links with the waterside gave it exotic and threatening sounds, smells and sights. Among its population were relatively high numbers of immigrant peoples, including Irish and Chinese. Lower George Street became Sydney's first Chinatown at the foot of The Rocks. The area hosted seamen from all over the world, some of whom took a liking to the place, married local women and settled there. Its culture was that of urban working people: drinking, pubs, gambling and sports dominated. Its distinctive rocky and steep topography and the increasingly old-fashioned, cheek-by-jowl houses were familiar and comfortable to residents. Still, they made journalists, do-gooders, philanthropists and readers feel ill at ease.

The Rocks were old Sydney, associated with the shadowy, shameful convict past. It seemed increasingly out of kilter with the present self-consciously modernising city. Even that significant improvement, the Argyle Cut, looked increasingly dark and menacing as the decades passed.

When the first epidemic of bubonic plague broke out in Sydney in 1900, all eyes turned to the old working-class waterfront neighbourhoods. The Rocks, in particular, were seen as the source of contagion. Fleas carried the disease on the rats that came ashore from ships, so people who worked in these areas were particularly vulnerable, and they bore the brunt of the disease. However, the plague affected many other parts of Sydney too, and of the 303 epidemic victims, only five were from The Rocks. Ironically, there had been significant improvements in urban conditions and amenities the decade before, and the infant mortality rate in the city wards had already dropped considerably.

Nevertheless, the plague catalysed the subsequent significant development in the area's history: the state government resumed the area around Darling Harbour in 1900, and the residents became public tenants. Over the next 20 years, the entire waterfront was demolished and rebuilt. In the residential areas, hundreds of houses were destroyed, so accommodation became harder for waterside workers' families who had to live near the piers. Neighbouring Millers Point was rebuilt with extensive public housing (some of the earliest examples in the world), although in The Rocks, the number of new houses fell far below what had been destroyed. It was hoped that industry and commerce would eventually sweep away the old houses and streets, and over the early twentieth century, large factories and stores did appear. Bushell's tea factory in Harrington Street, the State Clothing Factory and the Metcalfe Bond Stores, which still line George Street north, replaced earlier buildings but also provided work for local people.

From 1900, too, The Rocks were repeatedly scored and scarred. Whole streets of houses were demolished to make way for straighter street realignments, wharf developments, the Harbour Bridge approach in the 1920s and early 1930s, and the Cahill Expressway in the 1960s. But the local community did not disappear. Residences became the tenants of successive state government bodies; the Sydney Harbour Trust, the Maritime Services Board and the Sydney Cove Redevelopment Authority. This fostered the community, giving people tenure security and fixed rents for the first time. Instead of moving about every two years, as they had done in the nineteenth century, families stayed in one house over many years, even passing leases onto their children.

In some streets, such as Atherden Street, children grew up surrounded by grandparents, aunts and uncles. People felt they belonged in these houses and The Rocks; this sense of place would have essential outcomes. The completion of the Harbour Bridge also meant that The Rocks was bypassed by traffic and trade and became a forgotten enclave. The rate of local intermarriage has been high, and most Rocks people recall that everyone did know everyone.

The Rocks was a hardy perennial in the newspapers over the twentieth century, appearing in a succession of grand schemes dreamed up by planners and government departments, all involving complete demolition and redevelopment, none of which resulted. There were also nostalgic pieces that dwelt on the age and history of the neighbourhood, usually set in the context of imminent, inevitable change. Artists of the Old Sydney School sketched, painted and photographed the picturesque lanes and terrace houses, so different from the modern suburbs spreading around the city. By the early 1960s, curious tourists had begun to explore the old urban spaces. But to governments, The Rocks was a blot on the pride of the modern city; its terrace houses bore the stigma of slum buildings, and its people were considered slum dwellers. In December 1960, the state government advertised the whole area for sale in the New York Times; apparently, there were no takers.

In 1970, A new semi-autonomous body controlled the Rocks, the Sydney Cove Redevelopment Authority, headed by Colonel DO McGee. Colonel McGee was charged with efficiently relocating residents, often to outer-western Sydney, and redeveloping the area as a high-rise commercial precinct.

By this stage, many local people did not want to move, nor did they want The Rocks destroyed. The Rocks Residents Action Group, led by the determined and eloquent Nita McCrae, protested and lobbied. Still, when this proved ineffective, it asked the Builders Labourers Federation to help by placing a green ban on the area. Between 1971 and 1974, the green bans resulted in a bitter and often violent struggle known as the Battle of The Rocks. The green bans aimed to preserve the built fabric of the place maintain the community, and keep a place for working people in the city. In doing this, the residents, protesters and unionists were challenging the right of politicians and planners alone to shape the city's future.

They successfully defended the historic fabric from the wrecker's ball and bulldozer, but The Rocks had to pay its way. So, rather than remaining a working-class neighbourhood, it was developed by the Sydney Cove Redevelopment Authority as a historic attraction for tourists. As the local population aged and passed away, houses became shops, cafes and galleries. The old Argyle Bond Stores had already been converted to the Argyle Arts Centre, with its heady scents of handcrafted leather, soap and candles. After nearly 200 years of official suppression, the name was finally embraced in 1974 and listed with the Geographical Names Board as The Rocks. Publicity campaigns promoted tourism with the famous slogan: 'The Rocks: Birthplace of a Nation'.

Although historically dubious, this phrase caught the burgeoning public interest in Australian history, genealogy and heritage. The Rocks were now national heritage, so every Australian, not just that small number of residents, had a stake in the place.

One ironic outcome of the Battle of The Rocks is that today, only a handful of people live in the area, but more than 9 million people visit it yearly. Most tourists and day-trippers come to shop, eat and stroll, but some are pilgrims with deeply felt links to the place. They visit childhood homes or the sites where their forebears lived.

CHAPTER 2.

RAZOR GANGS AND PROSTITUTES

Push gangs of the earlier days were horses-asses of a different species. They were not barflies like those of the 1960s but lawless louts engaged in running warfare with other Sydney gangs of the time, such as the Straw Hat Push, the Glebe Push, the Argyle Cut Push, the Forty Thieves from Surry Hills and the Gibb Street Mob. They committed crimes like theft, assault and battery against police and pedestrians in the Rocks area. Female companions of the Push, called 'Donah's,' would entice drunks and seamen into dark areas to be assaulted and robbed by the gang.

Women were warned never to go near the Suez Canal; one of the most famous haunts of the Rocks Push was Harrington Place, also known as the "Suez Canal" (supposedly a pun on "sewers"), one of the most unsavoury places in Sydney in its time. there were stories of young women kidnapped and forced to work in brothels where the women were not much more than sex slaves.

The suburbs of Darlinghurst, Woolloomooloo and Kings Cross in Sydney in the late 1920s and early 1930s were a world in turmoil with vicious 'razor' gangs battling for control of the criminal underworld. They were called razor gangs because of the cutthroat razor (a straight shaving blade) that was the weapon of choice, especially after the Pistol Licensing Act of 1927, which meant automatic gaol time for anyone caught carrying an unlicensed firearm. The original Rocks Push gangs ran warfare with other Sydney gangs, such as the Straw Hat Push, the Glebe Push, the Argyle Cut Push, the Forty Thieves from Surry Hills and the Gibb Street Mob. They committed crimes like theft, assault and battery against police and pedestrians in the Rocks area. Female companions of the Push, called 'Donah's,' would entice drunks and seamen into dark areas to be assaulted and robbed by the gang. Good-natured women were warned never to go near the Suez Canal, **One of the most famous haunts of the Rocks. It was a different kettle of fish for the women of the street. The razor gangs at the heart of the war of 1927-31 were led by two women: Tilly Devine and Kate Leigh.**

Tilly Devine, known as the 'Queen of Woolloomooloo', ran a string of brothels centred around Darlinghurst and the Cross, particularly Palmer Street. Kate Leigh, known as the 'Queen of Surry Hills', was a sly groger and fence for stolen property. Tilly and Kate's battle for supremacy led to a running fight in the streets of Sydney that left many people dead, disfigured or doing gaol time.

Matilda Twiss was born in Camberwell, London, in 1900. She began working as a prostitute after she left school. Tilly was flirty, energetic, vigorous and pretty, soon earning good money. She met James Edward Devine in 1916, and it was a case of opposites attracting. Jim, or 'Big Jim' as he was known, was born in Victoria in 1892 and served as an Australian Digger in World War I. Jim was known to be sour and sullen and quick to temper. TIlly and Jim married in 1917 and soon had a son.

When Jim was repatriated home at the war's end, Tilly followed soon after, leaving behind her infant son to be raised by her parents. She arrived in Sydney on 13 January 1920 on the *Waimana,* a 'war bride' ship. Tilly is listed second from the top as Mrs M Devine. She soon began working as a prostitute in Sydney while Big Jim protected her. Tilly and Jim eventually divorced in 1943 after 25 years of marriage. Jim returned to Melbourne and died sometime in the 1960s.

By 1925, Tilly was well-known to police. In five years, she had accumulated a long list of convictions; the numerous offences ranged from common prostitution to indecent language, offensive behaviour and assault. The police report is a snapshot of Tilly's life leading up to 1925, which involved working the streets at night, clashes with police, lots of parties and heavy drinking.

Tilly served two years in the State Reformatory at Long Bay for maliciously wounding Sydney Corke with a razor blade. The stint inside convinced her to make significant career changes when released. She started her brothels rather than continuing as a street-walking prostitute. Tilly was able to pursue a long career as a madam because the law stated that it was only illegal for men to live off the earnings of prostitutes. She quickly set up several brothels around Palmer Street when released from gaol. Big Jim also started selling cocaine out of the brothels.

Kate Leigh, born in 1887, had a personal rivalry and enmity with Tilly that lasted for many years. They headed two of the most potent razor gangs and were out to protect their own. Kate ran a sly grog business that provided illegal alcohol after 6 p.m. when the pubs had to shut. Both women were rich, powerful, and violent and tried to outdo each other with furs and jewels. While Kate was a formidable adversary for Tilly, she had a generous side. She loved to be in court to see daily proceedings, sometimes bringing her vegetables to prepare for her evening meal.

On 22 June 1927, the original razor gangster, Norman Bruhn, was shot to death by a gunman lurking in the shadows outside Mac's sly-grog shop in Charlotte Lane, just around the corner from Stanley Street in Darlinghurst. Bruhn had come from Melbourne and formed the first razor gang, comprising 'Razor Jack' Hayes, George 'the Midnight Raper' Wallace and 'Snowy' Cutmore. They aimed to divest Tilly and Kate of their lucrative criminal enterprises forcibly, and for a time, they ran riot. 'Two women running crime in Sydney?' Bruhn had scoffed. 'How easy is this going to be!' Bruhn's razor men started ransacking Tilly's and Kate's premises and beating up their customers.

On his last day alive, Bruhn had spent the afternoon drinking at the Court House Hotel in Oxford Street, then caught a cab to Mac's. When he left, just after 10 p.m., he was shot down. When dying, true to the criminal code, Bruhn refused to name his assailant to the police, and his murderer was never apprehended. But the word on the mean streets of Darlinghurst was that Tilly Devine ordered Frank Green to pull the trigger.

Frank Green was born in Sydney in 1902. He became known as *The Little Gunman*, reflecting his stature of 1.65m. His gaol record shows that Green had brown hair and eyes, an L-shaped scar on his right cheek (a razor scar) and several bullet wounds on his body. Green worked as a gun for hire, and Tilly used him to protect her brothels in the late 1920s. Green had an explosive temper, not helped by the fact he was an alcoholic and cocaine addict. Green had a falling out with the Devines after the 1929 shooting of Gregory Gaffney, and he faded to obscurity before dying from stab wounds inflicted by his girlfriend in 1956.

From 1927 to the introduction of the consorting laws in 1930, Tilly Devine's and Kate Leigh's mobs went at each other. The women's criminal activities rarely overlapped, and while Tilly's stamping ground was Darlinghurst, Paddington, Woolloomooloo and Kings Cross, Kate's kingdom was headquartered in Surry Hills, but they had a fierce personal rivalry and genuinely despised each other. Each longed to be known as Sydney's unchallenged crime boss, with all the wealth, power, fear and headlines that status guaranteed.

Whenever Leigh or Devine gang members met, such as in Kellett Street in August 1929, there was a strong chance that violence would ensue. Kate would order the beating up and slashing of Tilly's men and women. Tilly's minions, in turn, ransacked Kate's grog shops and attacked her cocaine peddles in the Rocks. Kate stationed snipers with rifles on Surry Hills rooftops to ward off Tilly's troops. In Kate's pay were hair-trigger hoodlums like her lover Wally Tomlinson, Gregory 'the Gunman' Gaffney, Bruce Higgs, Bill 'the Octopus' Flanagan and Barney Dalton. Protecting Tilly's interests were her violent and drunken husband 'Big Jim' Devine (who shot Gaffney dead and is pictured below), Frankie 'the Little Gunman' Green (who dispatched Dalton), Guido Calletti, Sid McDonald, and the lethal, and beautiful, prostitute Nellie Cameron. At least six were slain in the Leigh–Devine gang wars and scores were maimed and wounded.

Former policewoman Peg Fisher spoke in an interview in 2000 about her first assignment, 70 years before, in 1930, to go out and gather information about Tilly and Kate. Peg told the reporter, 'In a lane near Palmer Street, Darlinghurst, I came face to face with Tilly. She was blocking the footpath, preventing me from proceeding. She said, "You're the new copper, ain't you? Well, you're not coming down this bloody street" She grabbed me and started shaking me. Next, a woman wearing a big black hat got off a tram. It was Kate Leigh. She approached where Tilly was shaking me like a rag doll and, without a word, she king-hit Tilly Devine and then sat on her in the road'.But Tilly could handle herself. Peg Fisher told the reporter, 'Oh, she was a dirty fighter and very strong. I saw her and Kate Leigh have a blue in Oxford Street. Tilly had Kate's hat off and was slapping her on the ground. Kate got much the worst of it.'

The notorious Guido Calletti was born in Sydney in 1902. He was in trouble with the law from the age of eight, and by the time he was 25, Calletti was the leader of the Darlinghurst Push, a small group of street brawlers and stand-over men. Calletti worked as a pimp, thief and hired thug, interspersed with work periods as a labourer and co-owner of a fruit barrow. Calletti had an ongoing love affair with Nellie Cameron (and rivalry with Frank Green), whom he eventually married in January 1934. Calletti died of gunshot wounds in 1939. There were many other notorious characters of criminal persuasion then too. Sid McDonald worked as a bodyguard for hire and was employed by Tilly at the height of the Razor gang wars. McDonald was born in Queensland in 1898, with minor charges and jail time. McDonald took part in the gunfight at Tilly's home in 1929 and reportedly died there. Then there was Nellie Cameron, born in 1912 on Sydney's North Shore. In 1926, she ran away from home and found work as a prostitute. Nellie was well known for her beautiful looks, sex appeal and hourglass figure. Her relationships with gangsters (and their deaths) Norman Buhn, Frank Green and Guido Calletti led to her becoming known as 'the Kiss of Death Girl'. Nellie Cameron eventually found love with an Irish seaman, but, convinced she had contracted cancer from bullet wounds sustained in her wild days, she died by her hand by gassing herself on 8 November 1953, aged 41, after outliving her gangster lovers. Nellie was buried as Ellen Katherine Bourke on 10 November 1953 in the Botany Roman Catholic Cemetery, now known as Eastern

Suburbs Memorial Park. Over 700 mourners attended her funeral, including Kate Leigh, Tilly Devine and ex-lover Frank Green.

On 17 July 1929, Kate Leigh's gang, led by Gregory Gaffney, ambushed Frank Green and Sid McDonald; the Devines, McDonald, and a wounded Green retreated to the Devine's Maroubra home, waiting for the next attack at midnight. Gaffney was shot dead by Big Jim. In Court, Jim stated he 'fired more to frighten' the assailants away than to harm. He was found not guilty of murder at his trial as he was protecting his property. Tilly filed for divorce from her husband Jim in 1942 after years of physical abuse. Their opposite personalities and hedonistic lifestyle finally took a toll on their relationship. Tilly went on to marry seaman Eric Parsons in 1945. Jim returned to Melbourne and died sometime in the 1960s.

In November 1926, Norman Bruhn, a standover man from Melbourne, arrived in Sydney and set up in the Cross. He came into conflict with Kate, Tilly and Phil, 'the Jew' Jeffs (who ran drugs and gambling in the Cross). Bruhn was shot dead in Surry Hills some six months later, possibly by Frank Green. In May 1929, a 'Battle of Blood Alley' in the Cross resulted in a 30-minute brawl between Jeffs and a rival gang. Jeffs was shot but recovered. Street violence Escalating street violence throughout the year when Frank Green and Sid McDonald were ambushed in Woolloomooloo by a group of Kate Leigh's men led by Gregory Gaffney. Devines, McDonald, and a wounded Green retreated to the Devine's Maroubra home, waiting for the next attack, which occurred at midnight. Gaffney was shot dead, while Tomlinson and Dalton survived. Big Jim, as usual, was found not guilty of murder at trial.

On 8 August 1929, the Battle on Kellett Street occurred while Kate was in gaol. Tilly was on the offensive and attacked Kate's sly grog shops in a pitched battle. On 5 September 1929, Big Jim and Frank Green shot Tomlinson and Dalton in the street. Dalton died, but Tomlinson survived and named only Green as his assailant. This was followed in January 1930 when Tilly was arrested as the *Vagrancy (Amendment) Act 1929* was enacted.

The Act attempted to curtail gang violence by giving Police new powers to arrest and target anyone habitually consorting with thieves, prostitutes or vagrants. Tilly promised the judge to leave Sydney for two years. In March 1930, The first of Green's murder trials started, but the jury deadlocked. Green was eventually acquitted at a second trial. Green has fallen out with Devines and no longer works for them. Both Tilly and Kate felt the effects of the Depression on their business and spent more time in gaol due to the Vagrancy Act. Kate was declared bankrupt in 1954 and died in 1964. By 1959, Tilly had to sell off her extensive property holdings to pay the Tax Office £20,000. She was left with only one brothel and her Maroubra house. Devine had suffered from chronic bronchitis for 20 years and died of cancer at 70 at the Concord Repatriation Hospital in Sydney on 24 November 1970. Her funeral service was held at the Sacred Heart Catholic Church, Darlinghurst. She was survived by a son she adopted during her second marriage. Her two children to Jim Devine had predeceased her.

CHAPTER 3.

THE DOWNTOWN PUSH

In my time of living the life of a drunk doing pub crawls along the hotel strip that was Sydney Rocks, The Royal George was the headquarters of the Downtown Push, usually known as just the Push... As well as the Libertarians and the aesthetes, there were the small-time gamblers, traditional jazz fans and the homosexual radio repairmen who had science fiction as a religion. The back room had tables and chairs. If you stuck your head through the back room door, you came face to face with the day's Push. The noise, the smoke and the diverse character of the humanity at the bar of facial expression state much to take in. It looked like a cartoon on which the best caricature artists of the press had all worked simultaneously, fighting for supremacy. Perhaps the most excellent cartoon character of all in those drinking sessions was a young buddy public servant with scruffy hair, a droopy moustache, a beer in one hand and Luck Strike cigarette in the other, dressed all in brown; a Corduroy shirt, jacket, stove pipe pants and suede shoes. I can hardly recognise that pompous ass of a self now, for all my views of life and living today is far removed from that scene. It was all an act, but in my blind alcoholism, I thought my shit didn't stink.

Sydney Libertarianism adopted an attitude of permanent protest recognisable in the sociological theories of the intellectuals of the day, Max Nomad, Vilfredo Pareto and Robert Mitchels, which predicted the inevitability of elites and the futility of revolutions. They used phrases such as "anarchism without ends", "non-utopian anarchism", and "permanent protest" to describe their activities and theories. Others labelled them as the 'futilitarians'. An early Marx quotation, used by Wilhelm Reich as the motto for his The Sexual Revolution, was adopted as a motto, viz:

[Since it is not for us to create a plan for the future that will hold for all time, all the more surely what we contemporaries have to do is the uncompromising critical evaluation of all that exists, uncompromising in the sense that our criticism fears neither its results nor the conflict with the powers that be. Quote unquote.] Most of those barflies stole quotes for intellectual comment, with self-opinionated righteousness, and added their viewpoint whilst full of piss and wind. This is the author's opinion. Quote, unquote.

Nevertheless, Push associates regularly assisted in organising and turning out for street demonstrations, e.g., against South African apartheid and in support of victims of the 1960 Sharpeville massacre against the initial refusal of immigration minister Alexander Downer. Sr., to grant political asylum to three Portuguese merchant seamen who jumped ship in Darwin and against Australia's participation in the Vietnam War.

In line with the Libertarians' rejection of conventional political models, electoral activism was foreign to the Push, save to urge non-voting and informal voting. At the election, after Prime Minister Harold Holt failed to return from a swim, artist and film-maker David Perry produced a highly acclaimed poster featuring "a continuum of pigs (inspired by Orwell's *Animal Farm*)" with the slogan "Whoever you vote for, a politician always gets in."

The most dramatic public event to impinge on the Push drinking opinions was the mysterious Bogle- Chandler (murder?) case of 1963 and its sequel, a heavily publicised inquest in which several Push personalities gave evidence. Another memorable incident involved discovering what news media recognised as a dismembered murder victim in an unlocked trunk at the foot of a city train station escalator. This was later revealed to be a collection of body parts, the property of a doctor, found and used in a macabre practical joke by a notorious confidence trickster, the late Julian Ashleigh Sellers (known in the Push as 'Flash Ash').[19]

The year 1964 saw the gradual demise of the Royal George Hotel as the prime focal venue of the Sydney Push, which dispersed its bustling social life to other traditional venues like the Newcastle, Orient and Port Jackson hotels in The Rocks and the Rose, Crown and Thistle at Paddington but also to alternative central-city pubs including the United States and Edinburgh Castle. By the early 1970s, the Criterion Hotel on the corner of Liverpool and Sussex Streets had become the watering hole of the last Push diehards. Meanwhile, Push hangers-on and 'tourists', now numbering hundreds, patronised pubs like the Four-in-Hand (Paddington) and the Forth and Clyde at Balmain, but these were venues of social entertainment, lacking the intellectual camaraderie, the informal folksong and the bohemian flavour of the Rock's 'George'.

The retired education professor Alan Barcan has published a personal account of his view of activism at Sydney University during the 1960s. Though he was not an eyewitness of Push's life, he provides some relevant insights into how student life became infected by Push's doctrines of freedom and rebellion to a point at which the social movement was superseded. Its leading personalities were dispersed or replaced with a new breed of social critics. This period saw the emergence of mainstream talents like poets Les Murray and Geoffrey Lehmann, journalists David Solomon, Mungo MacCallum (Jnr) and Laurie Oakes, **and Oz magazine** satirists Richard Neville, Richard Walsh and Martin Sharp, and maverick writer Bob Ellis. These people did not actively embrace the Push life but were strongly influenced by it.

Push personalities who emigrated to the United Kingdom included Clive James, Paddy McGuiness, Chester Philip Graham and Ian Parker, who returned to Sydney in the late 1970s and was knocked down and killed while drunk on Dixon Street. For some reason, a false account was promulgated that he died in a London street. Paddy McGuinness returned to Australia in 1971, working as a film critic, Labor ministerial staffer, right-wing newspaper columnist and journal editor until he died in 2007. Folksinger John Earls went to Bolivia, and former Tribune Communist newspaper cartoonist Harry Reade went to join Fidel Castro's revolution in Cuba and returned in 1971 at the same time as Paddy McGuinness. The disabled poet Lex Banning travelled to England and Greece from 1962 until 1964 but returned and died in Sydney in 1965. The folksinger Don Ayrton departed to settle in Queensland, where he committed suicide in 1982. A tragedy occurred as Paddy McGuinness departed for Italy by ship in May 1963. The farewelling crowd included a young Push lady, Janne (or Jan) Millar, who fell to the concrete dock floor from a height and suffered fatal head injuries. Several other tragic deaths occurred in this decade, including some from substance abuse, which was becoming a regular part of Sydney culture then.

Many young Push associates simply moved on to careers in the professions and academia. A reunion organised by André Frankovits at the Royal George/Slip Inn in 2000 attracted around 280. Another, at the Harold Park Hotel in February 2012, drew nearly 200, including some who had travelled from Hong Kong,

North Queensland and Perth to attend. Later annual re-unions have attracted around 50.

On the Push's demise, Anne Coombs stated: "[... things began to change] in 1964, the year the Beatles came and brought into the open that new phenomenon: 'youth culture'. Citing this, Alan Barcan added, "In advocating free love and opposition to authority, the Push and the Libertarians anticipated the new post-1968 morality. But society's adoption of many of their ideas undermined their *raison d'être*.

My Friday night drinking bouts with mates in the 1960s started at the German Wine cellar near Wynyard station. It sold beer in a Beer Stein. The publican served Schnitzler and cabbage with the drinks and a band somewhere in the background played the traditional festival drinking song 'Ein Prosit- 'a toast a toast of comfort' over and over every 15 minutes, so we were well fortified by the time we headed down George Street to join the drinkers at the back bar of Jim Buckley's Newcastle Hotel. Buckley had the pub at the south-west corner of George and Essex Streets from 1956 to 1972, and most of the creative drinkers of the day admired the painting of a nude figure of a Chloe-like character featured on one wall and other acclaimed artist work that adorned the rest. Most drinkers were wankers who were up themselves but pissed pots through and through.

Buckley took over as host and continued the tradition of former publican, Sydney actor, comedienne and silent film star Lily Molloy. Molloy starred opposite Snowy Baker in one of the earliest Australian films, "The Enemy Within". Lily Molloy transformed the Newcastle Hotel into one of Sydney's most popular bohemian pubs.

In the early 1970s, writer John Larkins and Bruce Howard, photographer, went on a 40,000km pub crawl around Australia, telling their wives, "Don't wait up!" With Larkin's beautiful words and Howards' fabulous photos, they chronicled a fantastic snapshot of Australian pub culture – many, both people and pubs, now gone.

Well, it took time for me to graduate to the drinking class of the Push and other nearby city bars of the 1960s and early 1970s, and by then, the old Push was a dread duck. Still, the reminisce of the old held fast with me, and to get there as a seasoned drunk, I needed to graduate. I got my grounding initially in the bush before my timely transfer to the city as a banker (and love-forsaken drinker) and then a stint in the public service for a few years before returning to the finance field.

Before the first quarter of 1963 was over, I was already on my way to my first transfer post for the Commonwealth Bank at Inverell on the New England Tablelands. As a stranger in town, I soon learned the local 'youth push.' My background growing up Catholic gave me a 'heads-up' to join the Catholic Youth Club. Little to do with being Catholic, it comprised young men and women over 18 who joined weekly social activities. Most of our clubs met regularly at a weekly dance in the Inverell town hall, or those who owned cars made their way to Glenn Innes to a local pub dance. It was an around 50 kilometres trip and a great way to get cuddle to and from the dance. Our weekend activities, when not racing cars, were to play a 'chicken-like' game with unsuspecting drivers. We would meet at a service station outside town limits and choose a car with external door handles.

When the driver pulled up for petrol, one 'pillion passenger ' would attach the right hand to the left-hand front passenger door handle. When the driver took off heading townward, the 'rider' learned out with the grip arm bent and knees leaning against the vehicle's body. As the car picked up speed, the rider began straightening the grip arm, leaning outward. Once the rider was in danger of losing grip, the idea was to lean back in and knock on the passenger window with a face appearing there. Apart from scaring the hell out of the driver, it always resulted in a sudden stop. Nobody got hurt, but it was dangerous fun.

In the winter months, I managed to get a run in 2nd Grade with the local Rugby Union team. They were fun trips playing rugby in various townships in New England. As usual, we would adjourn to the bar when the game finished. The habit of indulging in too many heavy drinking sessions was the norm for socialising and a daily after-work pastime for us bankers. I had not realised it then, but alcoholism already had its grip on me from the moment I took my first sip of beer. My infatuation with a quiet, dark-eyed beauty during my daily banking routine made it hard to concentrate on my daily duties in my year in Inverell. Desire became an obsession and ultimately a progressive realisation of a worthwhile pre-determined goal.

So for a time, Pricilla, in passion, was my constant companion; with her, many an evening was spent fogging up the windows of my car. As for my driving, it was reckless at the best of times. On a trip to the movies at Delungra one evening in her Dad's car, we were in a passionate embrace as I sped along a dirt road to paradise. In my enthusiasm to complete more than one task at a time, I had inadvertently taken my eyes off the road and missed an approaching bridge. We flew through the air ending squarely in the middle of a dry creek bed. Fortunately, the country was in drought, and the creek was as dry as a drunk tonging for a drink.

Pricilla and I maintained our passion without so much as a fibrillation of a heartbeat. Dead on, we drove along the creek bed to find a way out and back on the road again. Usually, my small two-seated sports car was not conducive to the passionate embraces we needed, thus ending our regular embrace with sore backs. It gave me some joy to take her Dad's car for a spin. Besides, it had a column gear change in contrast to the awkwardness of the gear stick in my little sports car. The only other incident in Priscilla's affair that put pay to me using the family car was a weekend on the Gold Coast. Somewhere in our crossing into Queensland, we drove along the beachfront and pulled over onto the beach's edge to celebrate our arrival. Oblivious to the fact that the car was slowly sinking into the sand, into the rhythm method. Unable to open the doors, I climbed out of the window and enlisted the help of some young surfer types. The boys were out on a late-night drinking spree and, in good humour, helped me lift the car back to a stable surface. Meanwhile, Pricilla sat starry-eyed in a haze, watching the proceedings unfold.

Our relationship came to a rather abrupt end not long after I was transferred to Coffs Harbour. I was still on the road to rack and ruin, driving like a love-sick maniac from Coffs to Inverell at weekends and return. Around that time, I put my car into a spin on the journey west and took out a guidepost. In the revision mirror, I noticed the guide post flying through the air, for in my haste I struggled to keep the car on the road. Dirt roads in drought can be a godsend for a young driver as the loose gravel saves the car from flipping. I now recall that I always succeeded in dangerous situations whilst driving, on this occasion hammering that machine towards infinity. The romance died the day a mate's mother gave me the Inverell times to read. Pricilla's photo appeared larger than life with her new husband. It was her wedding day, not three weeks after we had separated. It appears she had been two-timing me all along. That girl had an insatiable appetite for lust.

I had driven the one-hour journey on the first Saturday morning of a new economic means of exchange to my hometown, for decimal currency took over from pounds, shillings and pence that week. On my return trip to Coffs Harbour, I passed a 'land for sale' sign. It was for a new subdivision at nearby Valla Beach, about eight clicks north of Nambucca Heads. I went to the Real Estate Agent next door to the only business in Valla Beach then. A General store for emergency supplies, milk bar, Post Office and Estate Agency all rolled into one. The sign in the window showed the land price in the old currency at five hundred pounds per block. Considering I saved three thousand pounds, I could have easily purchased six blocks. I went to the beachfront to view the small estate of eight blocks. However, I had changed my mind when I reached the outskirts of Coffs. The money was burning a hole in my mind, and I needed to do something with it other than see the figures on my savings bank savings passport. So I went to Kempsey the following weekend to sink most of my hard-earned savings into a previous owner, 62 EK Holden. My father had come along to inspect my pending purchase and gave it the once-over approval before I parted with my money. I was in my element; it had a column gear change and would suit my carnal desires.

My final year with the Bank was in Liverpool in Sydney. It was the fourth most significant branch of the Commonwealth Bank and had staff union issues from the day of my arrival. That year, the Union visited the Bank Premises on eighty occasions with employer-employee issues. A pig of a man who shall remain nameless to allow his soul to remain at peace was the bane of every young staff member. In my case, he followed me like a shadow whilst at work, in my lunch hour and sometimes before work. By the time I resigned from my services to banking, I was a sleepless, nervous wreck. The bank's secret service man stood in the shadows whilst I ate my lunch, adjourned to the bar for a beer or attempted to escape into the arms of another lover. I was appointed 'Teller One ' in a series of eight tellers in that branch.

Liverpool was a growth suburb but still had the appeal of something out of the Wild West at the time. It was near the end of the train line for city commuters. It had a large working-class population of city office workers, Italian market gardeners, small retail businesses, car dealers, and one of Sydney's first large shopping centres. The township had a consistent bus and train service and was a stone's throw from Bankstown airport. The suburb grew westward with housing and farms as far away as Macquarie Field. There was also a new housing commission estate at Cabramatta for the not-so-rich dependent upon shopping in Liverpool.

Nearby, Heathrow housed a large Army base for which we were responsible for servicing everything money-related. That was apart from our Friday night duty as bankers to visit the new migrant hostel at Heathrow, mainly filled with"Ten-pound Pom" arrivals. It was always Friday night fever for us. The job was to collect the pay from those tin hut dwellers, stamp their Commonwealth Bank passbooks as proof of their diligent saving, return to the bank around nine p.m., and lock the loot into the safe. The musicians at the migrant camp were often practising on our arrival there. The young English lads, the 'Easybeats,' belted out "Friday on my mind" as we counted their parent's meagre savings. At my height of achievement in banking, I graduated from the job of Teller 1 to Savings Bank Examiner. The last post was trumpeting out my banking death note. It was no mean feat for a seemingly average student who scrapped through intermediate math to reach such dizzy heights of banking, but I had switched off from my banking career prospects.

I felt like I would crack but did not realise then that my 'SS shadow' and Management had grand plans for me up the ladder in the CTB banking system. I was doing an excellent job for them but was possibly far too young to take on the responsibility I found myself in, shackled with a hectic banking environment. I had decided to take a break and tendered my resignation on my holiday return. The big boss pleaded good reason for me to stay on and suggested another holiday, but I had already decided. I did not know what I wanted to do; I just wanted out of the restrictions of white-collar work and the artificial greetings of Mr, Sir and Madam.

I applied to Qantas to join the Fight Steward training with visions of international travel in the back of my mind. The first interview I breezed through and was called back a week later to attend a final selection. In front of me sat three men who plied me with questions relating to current affairs, international events and finally, a question on two articles I had read in the daily press that day that had caught my attention. As luck would have it, I had read the headlines and the feature cartoon on the way to the interview. I passed with flying colours and was immediately sent to the Qantas GP for a once-over. The only block to my career prospects was my height. The minimum height for flight stewards back then was 5' 7", and I was 5'6.5" barefooted. Fortunately, I didn't have to take off my shoes for the examination, and my boots had at least a half-inch heel, so I made it.

There was a fortnight's gap before I would get the confirmation of acceptance and joining date, so I had to find something to do. I was in a new romantic relationship and having some fun in drinking sprees with a couple of my banking mates, but I needed some cash flow to get by with food, clothing and shelter in the meantime. I was living in a boarding house at Mount Druitt then and had used my payout from the bank to pay a couple of week's rent in advance, but apart from some petrol monies, I had none.

Waiting for Qantas' final job acceptance, I visited my Cousin Kay at the engineering section of RK radio. As quickly as a flash, I was offered a job there mainly due to Kay's influence as an Exempt Technician Assistant. When I got acceptance confirmation, I threw in the Qantas opportunity and opted to stay with this new part-time job. Typical of reckless youth, I could not see the wood from the trees.

The Engineering section was a part of the then PMG, but the job was fantastic. Whilst my initial intention was to stay for the two weeks before joining Qantas, all that changed when I met the Head of Engineering, John Day. He took a shine to me and offered me a permanent post as his designated full-time driver, chief cook, and bottle washer. My initial duty was to build him an Engineering library. He had enquired if I had any idea how to do that. My immediate reply was, "Yes, Mr. Day," although I did not have a clue, I accepted the challenge.

Once he had returned to his office, I went looking for the best person to give me the right advice within the Engineering works. I was soon pointed in the direction of the Senior Technician with the most clues. He quickly picked out a file and a binder and explained the A to Z procedure for recording and filing all matters relating to engineering. He even produced a wooden cabinet with shelving which he said I could use to house the new library, which I figured would do the job just fine. Armed with this information, a template of the filing procedure, and a leather-bound file, I set to work. The money and resources to achieve my task were no issue. Thanks to my cousin Kay's connections, it was after all the Public Service and funds were released within 24 hours. I had the whole engineering library documented in neat files, much like CTB savings bank files. In hindsight, I had unknowingly duplicated the CTB system. John Day was genuinely impressed, and as a reward, he gave me a PMG Utility as my vehicle to use on and off the job.

Under John Day's tutelage, I took the role and title of Acting Senior Technician when Seniors Tech took his annual four-week leave. Officially the PMG would not have allowed an unqualified person to do that gig, but I had The Man as my connection. It was another of those straightforward roles, recording all the statistics for the Country TV powers of Little Brother Mountain, Big Brother Mountain and one other up on the North Coast. The daily signal recording and graphing task was laborious, but I completed the task without a hitch. The admin; then sent in my high-duty payment sheet, kindly endorsed by John Day, and my pay rapidly increased.

My duties changed from administration to being on call for any just-in-time delivery work that took the man's fancy or was considered essential to the department's needs. One day I would attend duties at the ABC Television Station with a technician at Gore Hill in St. Leonards. The next I was on my way with him to Moruya to check out the Australian Broadcasting Commission tower with John Day, the boss himself. On another, I would be climbing a T.V. tower with a technician to check out some problems with the signal. Back then, the PMG, which later became

Telstra, was responsible for all technical equipment for radio, T.V. cable and phone lines.

Our area was focused on TV as it was our responsibility to expand the network in that decade of the 1960s. Not only TV Stations and towers had to be completed and maintained, but booster stations for country areas were also our responsibility.

CHAPTER 4.

WORKING THE ALCOHOLIC MIND

I was in what was called the fourth division of the public service. The then PMG employed technicians responsible for TV equipment, radio and telephone exchanges, the linesmen and techs who maintained the on-street equipment and the Primary Works Department for underground cable. In my time in the PMG, I graduated to work in all those areas.

At this time, I was asked to assist a newly appointed Russian engineer, and a trainee was on loan from NSW University for practical experience in the field. As for the practicality of the intended Engineering task, things didn't go strictly as intended. Alex, the Russian Engineer, was, for all intention purposes, an accident waiting to happen. Once appointed to the PMG and our department, he decided to go for his driving licence. Alex had attempted it multiple times and failed repeatedly. It got to the stage that the Police were afraid to ride with him because he was too erratic and a danger to himself and the travelling public. Alex finally obtained his licence by bribing a cop at the Redfern police station. He had purchased a new VW Beetle and was travelling on his merry way from Redfern Police Station back to our city as a first-day licence holder. He never made it out of Redfern. One hundred metres up the road from the Police station Alex lost control of the car, wiping out three telephone boxes. Those little red telephone boxes stood on the main route where the pedestrian flow was at its peak. The phones hung from the back of the box with a coin slot attachment for payment of the call. Redfern had three side-by-side and was close to the Redfern railway station. They were bright red and could be seen from a long distance on the ground and, for that matter, from out space too. It was unusual to find an empty one, and people wishing to make a call usually had to line up and wait for an empty cubical. God must have been on the side of the telephone users as, on this rare occasion, the three phone boxes were empty just when Alex came beetling along. He didn't slow for a fraction of a second and neatly took out the three boxes and totally wrote off his beetle. The police were on the scene in minutes, and Alex lost his licence on the spot. The PMG covered up the incident, but Redfern remained without three public telephone boxes from that day forward. I never realised then how dangerous the world would become within the next 24 hours.

The next day was Saturday and Alex the Russian, David, the trainee engineer and a clueless Tech's Assistant, namely me, left Mascot on a plane bound for Dubbo loaded with technical equipment for fieldwork. We were to do area strength measurements for Television in the Pilliga Scrub, between Narrabri and a distant tower near Coonabarabran. We arrived at Dubbo airport Avis car hire counter to arrange a car for a week's hire to complete our assigned tasks.

Alex completed the paperwork, and the receptionist requested Alex's driver's licence. In a semi-demanding tone, he turned to me and requested my driver's licence, making some excuse that he left his home in Sydney. I took responsibility for the car hire and the driving of same. I had been taught never to question a boss's reasons for a work duty. However, I did question Alex after we left the counter; although he had the authority over me, I was taken aback by the fact that I ended up with the vehicle responsibility and driving duty. It was then that Alex came clean about his loss of licence. It was no more than five minutes into the trip into town when Alex insisted on driving.

The streets of Dubbo were deserted except for one young teenage girl wandering along the main street. I asked Alex to stop; winding down my window, I asked the young women for the location of the hotel we had booked for the night. She replied, pointing in the general direction. "Well, you take a f**ken left at the next corner, then take the next on the f**ken right, and it's on the next f**ken corner." I thanked her for her explicit clarity of direction, and we journeyed onward. Once we had booked in and dropped our gear in our rooms, we headed for the bar.

Thus began our week of continuous drinking, driving across the country, setting up equipment, climbing a T.V. tower and flirting with danger in a small aircraft. The morning after the night before, we left the Dubbo hotel on a mission to get to Coonabarabran T.V. tower before the local studios began the early morning programme. Alex was behind the wheel in our Avis Ford Falcon rent. The RTA had recently completed a duel expressway **and** David the trainee Engineer and I had both fallen asleep as soon the car gained some speed on the long straight stretch of road, due in part to our heavy drinking session the night before. Alex seems to be coping behind the wheel even though he downed copious quantities of vodka the evening before whilst we matched him drink for drink with beers.

A sudden bump in the vehicle caused me to wake up fully alert to the situation. Alex was driving with his foot hard on the accelerator, head down, trying to tune in the radio. He had inadvertently turned the steering wheel without realising he had done so, too intent on his need to hear a radio broadcast.

The impact of hitting the edge of the road had woken me; undeterred, Alex, from his radio tuning activity, was heading straight for a guidepost. I threw myself to the driver's side grabbing and turning the wheel as I did so. The vehicle spun sideways, narrowly missing the guide post and heading at full speed down the expressway. Alex, now altered to the situation, clutched the steering with both hands in a vice-like grip and hung on. The tyres suddenly gained a temporary grip on the road, and I was catapulted like an arrow halfway out the passenger door window. I grabbed both inside supports and, with my upper body being forced to-ward the road surface, yelled at Alex to let go of the wheel.

I trusted the vehicle would right itself by sheer momentum, but it was not to be, as Alex's hands were glued solid to the steering. The back rear passenger side tyre was almost off its rim, and I prayed it would not blow. Just as suddenly, the vehicle gained road traction and sped across the double-lane highway, with me still yelling at Alex to let go of the steering well. The immediate effect was to send me flying back into the passenger seat.   It was to no avail; the vicelike hold of the prominent Russian remained tight on the steering with a right-hand lock grip. The vehicle left the road still doing top speed as Alex held the steering tight, but his right foot was complex upon the accelerator. The Falcon went airborne across a barbed wire fence as livestock and cowering crows scattered, and the car headed up a slight slope and lodged between two trees. David, in the back seat, had bounced around the cabin. Alex sat in a daze with hands still vice-like on the steering wheel. It was a time before seat belts became mandatory in all vehicles, so 'knuckling down and buckling up" was not an option. Miraculously no one was injured.

We quickly assessed the situation and realised that apart from slight damage below the door line of the car, all was fine and dandy. The mud caked below the door base was our saving grace. The recent rain and soft paddock had cushioned our flight and rough landing. All that remained was to get across the paddock and to the expressway again. After calling Alex "A bloody idiot" several times, David and I took charge of the situation. Alex bus-ied himself, taking photos of the car between the two trees. We managed to push the car over a slight slope, and as luck would have it, the area was stony, and there was a break in the fence.

The vehicle started without a hitch, and with me now insisting, I took over driving duties, consciously aware that the vehicle was hired in my name.

In haste, we arrived at the TV equipment technician's office just before our appointment. Alex agreed with the T.V. studio to show test patterns to replace standard programs for three-minute intervals at agreed time slots during the next week of programmes. We intended to drive within a 200 km radius of the T.V. tower and signal to do some area strength measurements with our on-board equipment when the test patterns appeared on the screen. We were to test the signal and record our findings back to PMG RK radio for their decision as to a booster station or a further T.V. tower to be installed, based on the findings of our measurements.

Once we had breakfast and a couple of beers at the local pub, we set off for our first lot of experiments about 50 km from Coonabarabran township. We completed four experiments within a 50 Km circumference around the tower and, all in all, did some 300 km by nightfall, returning to the pub for a late dinner and adjourning to the bar for a further drinking spree. The pub allowed us to drink beyond their 10. O'clock closing. By 11. p.m. We had made our way to bed, and I was out cold after a belly full of beer with rum chasers. Alex returned to his room with a bottle of vodka!

The very next morning, we headed out early, a little worse for wear as we had arranged for the first test pattern of the day to be at 8. a.m. on the dot for three minutes. We set our plan to do four tests on the day at a circumference of 100 km each apart from the T.V. tower. The equipment took about ten minutes to set up, three minutes to record the signal and ten to pack up and head to the following location. We repeated the same experiment equidistant from the tower at all compass points. The process worked well despite the heat of the day and the pests of little flies. We made significant progress and had three more days of testing to complete our work. Surprising with my young driver skills on the dirt roads, but ever mindful of a current T.V. road safety advert "Young drivers are most skilled, but they are also the most killed," I play it safe into corners and only gunned the car on the straight. We were safely back in the bar in the late afternoon for another drinking session.

The Publican arranged for the pub to provide our dinner, and drinks flowed until closing. Around closing time, I was well in my cups, as was David. Alex, a little unsteady of hand, had tied a handkerchief around his neck to hold the glass without shaking whilst drinking another vodka. I had never realised until then how much Russians loved their Vodka. We staggered from the bar with a repeated sleep pattern. We all slept in and didn't get to breakfast until 8. a.m. The pub had just cracked their line of kegs and was testing the beer, so we helped them with the test.

Outside the pub, Alex insisted on taking a photo of us drinking underneath the town monument and clock. The clock struck 9, and we missed the first test pattern at the nearby TV Tower. The publican obliged us with a photo on Alex's camera, drinking a beer with the hands of the clock providing proof of the time of our morning reviver. Our next point if the compass reading was 150 km away at 11 o'clock. So we hightailed it into the Pilliga Scrub with time to spare and set up the equipment covered again with annoying little flies. They were in our eyes, nose and ears, nearly driving us mad. I had made up my mind right then and there to apply for a permanent clerical appointment in the Third Division of the Public Service to further my career. I concluded I was too educated to remain seated on a metal box in the middle of nowhere doing what seemed useless work experiments. Besides I was not qualified and was only a temporary employee and didn't want to pursue a technical career. I could see myself climbing the administrative ladder supporting university-educated academics or some such.

Meanwhile, we still had two more experiments to do before dark at the appointed times with the TV station, so we set forth in the scrub to the North West for the two rendezvous as planned. We had already recorded that the first experiment of the day had failed. Another night of drinking was taking its toll on us, but keen to get the job finished we were up bright and early before the heat of the day got the better of us and more importantly to beat the flies. We had to do the 200 km circumference in four experiments at all points of the compass. It was a long trip to the first sight for the test and we managed to get a weak signal for about a minute of the three on the test pattern. It was then that Alex came up with a bright idea.

Well on paper it seemed that way to go, but in reality, it proved costly to the PMG and a failure. Alex had the notion that if we hired a pilot and a plane we could rig up an antenna on the aircraft wing. In so doing send a signal to the equipment on the ground at the base of the TV tower and use a range finder from there to gauge the distance of the plane to the tower. Thus, the measurements could be recorded without any further need for field experiments.

So We set off to Dubbo to hire what we needed. We contracted a pilot who's working for a crop dusting company and got an agreement to use the company's Piper Comanche aircraft for our purposes. 'Dangerous Dan' the pilot, we later found out, had been grounded by Qantas for a year for low flying over a private beach as a dare, and wiped out a fence scaring the hell out of a farmer cattle herd whom he vowed later could not be milked for weeks after Dan's flying stunt. The farmer phoned Civil Aviation with an official complaint and our illustrious Pilot was caught red-handed. He had landed the commercial plane neatly at Mascot on a training flight but the barbed wire and a fence post wrapped around one wing gave him away. So to fill in the year during his grounded from his Qantas, Dan accepted a job as a crop duster at Dubbo. Alex the crazy Russian Engineer enlisted the help of 'Dangerous Dan' to drill a hole in the top of the right wing of the aircraft and feed a connection back to the plane for the unproven experiment.

David and I headed to town in search of a Range Finder and as luck would have it we found a disposal store and hired an old army one, using Alex's expense account credit card to pay. On our return to the aircraft, Alex was waiting for us. It was all set up for the Pilot to fly outwards from the TV tower at Coonabarabran mountain top. The Pilot was instructed to turn on the equipment at a pre-determined time and fly in circle patterns outward from the tower, increasing the distance with signals from the ground and a mud map drawn by Alex with the appropriate distance for the flight pattern included. We felt pleased with Alex's plan of action for the next morning and were back in the bar a little earlier than planned to take up where we left off our drinking session from the night before. Early the next morning, despite hangovers, we were up on the mountain top twigged the equipment linking with the nearby TV signal getting first-class reception. Now, it remained a simple matter to meter a corresponding signal from the aircraft to the ground equipment. David and I had the dubious duty to climb the tower with the range finder and quote the distance the aircraft was circling its way around the tower, advising Alex who recorded the signal strength below. My job was to support David a couple of rungs below him, yelling the Range Finders reading to Alex. I was relieved that I had only to climb halfway up that skeleton of steel, hanging in the wind on that manmade structure in the sky above the mountain top. The flight pattern and signals worked ok for the nearest experiment but the communication broke down between the pilot and Alex for the distant circles, so we had to abandon day 1 of the experiments. We adjourned to the bar mapping out a plan for the next day.

It was agreed for David to go up in the plane with the Pilot the next day and gauge the distance from the plane to the tower, increase that distance at pre-arranged times with the aid of binoculars and Range Finder, advising the Dangerous Dan of his next move. My job was to assist Alex with the equipment on the ground and signal the plane to move out further from the tower for the next round of test pattern signals. It meant that David had to the car trip to Dubbo and back to the disposal store for the hire of strong binoculars for our next level of experiments. Our usual drinking session continued as we mapped out the next day's activity. We were all up bright and early as David drove Alex and me up the mountain to the stored equipment and headed off to Dubbo for his assigned task. He was to return back to us after returning to Dubbo airport with "Dangerous Dan" at the controls of the Piper.

All seemed to work okay for some of the closer experiments, but as soon as we attempted to do the distant ones we lost the plane's signal. It proved a frustrating day and as Dangerous Dan was running short of fuel the plane turned back and he tipped the wing to let us know he was on his way home.

Alex via a telephone to the airport spoke to Dan on his return to base and suggested the boosting of the battery charge on the PMG apparatus as it was apparent that the gear was low on signal and was showing a red light on the ground equipment. It was just a matter of putting the battery on an overnight battery system to get full charge strength for the planned signal. We agreed with Alex that he should return to Dubbo in the morning to ensure all was ready for the last try at completing the desired test results.

David and I had a week's worth of signal experience, we were appointed by Alex to take over the duty of recording the metered signals below the tower the next day. The plan was for Alex to drive to Dubbo to fly back to the tower with 'Dangerous Dan' to complete the tasks ahead. I mused to myself which was the greater risk, Alex driving the car on the expressway he had lost control of or riding with the Maverick grounded Qantas pilot flying around the country skies. Little did I know then, the tide would turn and I was out to be plunged into that danger zone. We were awake bright and early after another night of drinking. David met me at breakfast, he like me was keen to have the morning-cooked breakfast of bacon, eggs and baked beans on toast with copious amounts of tea to get our body back in shape. Alex appeared at the doorway looking worse for wear. He had been vomiting convulsively throughout the night and was in no shape for the drive to Dubbo, let alone flying with 'Dangerous Dan.' So it was agreed that I would take the wheel and drive to Dubbo to be the pillion passenger on the plane for the final day's duties. Alex had figured that he would be all right to do the groundwork up on the mountain top and he gave me some final instructions as to what to check on the plane. I had a list to ensure the antenna was intact on the wing, the wiring inside the plane was connected to the antenna, and the signal equipment and the battery were at full charge. Armed with these instructions, I dropped off my follow-drinking companions at the top of the mountain and headed for Dubbo.

Dan was waiting for me and seemed a little annoyed but patiently awaited as I checked and rechecked the list of items as instructed by Alex before we taxied out for take off. The ride was smooth and strangely peaceful as we flew high above the clouds. It was a cloudy day with low fog partly obscuring the TV Tower from our view on the plane. Dan flew the circuit a few times but no signal was to be heard, so he got my approval to give up and head for Dubbo airport.

Halfway through the return flight, Dan enquired: "We have a full tank of fuel on board, and the PMG has not stopped paying for it anyway, so do you mind if we have a little fun now?" I said, " Sure," and Dan replied: " I will show you what we are not allowed to do under aviation rules as a pilot." He pointed ahead to a black cloud ahead and headed the aircraft in that direction. "We cannot fly deliberately into unknown territory beyond our designated flight plan." Dan headed deep into the cloud, and we suddenly went from daylight to darkness like a train in a tunnel. Daylight appeared soon enough, and we were back on course again. We returned to a pleasant sunlit day as we rode silently towards Dubbo airport. I thought that was the end of Dan's idea of fun until we flew above a large country estate. I remarked how beautiful the property looked from our bird's eye view of the sky. Dan's "Where?" was answered, and by my signal pointing downward from my pillion passenger window. It was all Dan had been waiting for: "Let's have a look" he said. Dan leaned the joystick to the right and forward, and the plane began to shudder and make an eerie sound as we dived like a fighter plane ready to mix it with the Bloody Red Baron of Germany.

The rooftop of the homestead was fast approaching as we headed towards ground zero. At the last second, Dan pulled back on the joystick and turned the plane left as it roared its way back skyward. That was not the end; Dan had danger in his eyes now. He quickly retorted, "Brace yourself," turning the plane upside down as we climbed and did a belly roll back upright. I was relieved to see the Dubbo airport below. Dan grounded the aircraft, and I descended a little unsteady on my feet. My face must have looked as green as the pastures of Ireland. Dan had a stupid grin on his face as I fought back the desire to throw up. Back in control mode and in the airport hangar with Dan, I said goodbye as I grabbed his hand for a final handshake." We had some fun, didn't we?" were his final parting words. I was feeling better and, now raising a grin, said, "Yeah and good luck getting your suspension lifted with Qantas." I never did catch his surname, but every time I board a Qantas flight and hear the Captain say," Good Morning, this is Captain Dan…" I wonder if it's him and say a quiet prayer that the plane doesn't go into a belly roll in flight or head towards earth in a nosedive. I did not know then that some year later, I would find myself on a drinking spree with Dangerous Dan, in my capacity as a writer on the Rocks in Sydney town.

Back in Coonabarabran, we collected our bags and headed for Dubbo again. A hot shower, a few beers and a good night's sleep were what I longed for now. Alex was still sick, as was David, and they both lay on their respective beds hoping for a speedy recovery. I was feeling grand and visited their motel room. In his wisdom, Alex had kindly swapped his room with me and moved into a twin-share room with David. I looked at them both in their misery, remarking: " You guys are weak." Famous last words as I headed for the motel swimming pool to do a couple of laps and cool off again before bedtime. On arrival at Mascot mid-Saturday afternoon, I said goodbyes to my intrepid travelling companions. I was keen to catch up with my then-girlfriend and head out to Parramatta Golf Club for a night of drinking and dancing.

Esther, the beautiful blue-eyed blond, greeted me with a passionate embrace. I felt like Omar Sharif embracing Julie Christie in " Dr.Zhivago." Such feelings didn't last long as I began to drink my first and only schooner at the Parramatta Golf Club that night. Feeling an attack of vomiting coming on, I rushed to the toilet and did just that. I emerged some minutes later in a confused state, with extreme loss of coordination and difficulty breathing. I handed my car keys to Esther, and she began to drive me back to her home near Bankstown. The journey was slow as I needed to stop frequently to throw up. When we reached Burwood, I had to ask her to stop at a pub, and I headed for the bar downing a Port wine and Brandy mix to settle my stomach. It was useless, and Esther headed the car towards the nearest hospital at Summer Hill and the Emergency ward.

A night stay in the hospital, intravenous feeding of a Saline solution, and some drugs to settle my stomach did the trick. The night sheet at the end of the bed read 'Alcoholic poisoning.' It was no wonder after a long trail of heavy boozing for a week. I should've seen it coming and taken this event as a final warning sign, but a lifetime ahead of alcoholism awaited me in the future. Who can foresee? I was young and considered myself bulletproof.

Monday morning, Alex, David and myself on the red carpet to give our report on the designated assignment we had endeavoured to complete. Alex had two neat files ready to present his case to the PMG Engineering Department regarding the area strengths measurements outcome and the other file for the Divisional Clerk's stamp of approval of the excessive expenditure on our given assignment from the previous week's activity. Alex's file showed the area surveyed for the experiments and the record of every experiment that had a positive result and those that didn't. He even included the one we failed to attend when we slept in. It was filed as a failed experiment which should have been recorded as 'N/A,' not in attended! He justified the recording of one successful experiment at the furthest distance from the tower and recorded the aeroplane idea as abandoned because of storm interference.

CHAPTER 5.

LIVING THE LIFE OF RILEY

Regarding the overblown costings of our journey into the wilderness, Alex had neat columns of figures right down to the last drink. He backed this all up with the photographs of the car incident with photographs of the car lodged between two trees, the undercarriage image done to the Avis hire car, shots of us all drinking at the clock tower at 9 a.m., night shots of us drunk at the bar with strategically placed files of statistics at the bar to give the impression we were still working and not just on the booze. The aeroplane hire was backed up by photos of preparing the equipment for installation, including the antenna on the wing, the signal system in the plane, equipment under the tower for recording signals and a couple of photos of David and me up the tower. Morrie, the Divisional Clerk, listened to Alex's explanation with a severe look and a steel gaze. When Alex, at last, ran out of wind, Morrie took the file and, with a smile, spread across his dial: "Best we forget about this file and expenses; we will find another way to write it all off." he said. And with that, he took all the photos, put them in his top drawer, and shot the film of Alex's hard work in recording costs into the waste paper bin under his desk. It would not be the last time I experienced money wastage by the Engineering Departments of the P.M.G.

The Monday week after our return from the bush, everything had returned to routine. I took the opportunity after John Day had returned to his office from a field trip, before he learnt of the boozing week with my intrepid travellers at Coonabarabran, to announce to him my intention to complete the Public Service examination for entry into the 3rd Division of the PMG. John was very understanding even though it would be the end of our association at RK Radio, and me being his right-hand man. My job as a lowly temporary 4th DivisionTech's Assistant and personal dog body for John Day was ending. He was most understanding and invited me to join him at lunch up the road, on the corner of Pitt and Park streets, where the Water Board had an in-house restaurant on the second floor. Once we had lunch, I joined John to ride the lift up to the top floor. It turns out his father was the head of the Water Board at the time, and he just wanted to introduce me to him. On the way down the lift, he explained. "When you are accepted into the 3rd Division of the Public Service, you will have a choice as to which branch of the service you wish to work, so should you choose the Water Board, Dad will be a good contact.

The PMG is possibly the best example of the order of workings. The 4th Division comprises all the exempt personnel like me, clerical assistants, not clerks, exempt staff being non-permanent, permanent technicians and their assistants, senior technicians, line inspectors and linesmen who worked in the pits for laying wiring for telephones and coaxial cable for long-distance connections. The third division comprised engineers and clerks with different rankings from clerk class 1 to clerk class 9. The 2nd Division comprised those immediately under the Post Master General from technical to administrative. The Post Master General himself is a 1st Division Public Servant. The same pecking order applied to the Post Office from the 4th Division Postman to Post Office staff and, in turn, up the ladder to the Post Master General. Every Department of the Public Service has the same levels of order. The Taxation Commissioner, The Attorney General, and every other head of a Government organisation are 1st Division Public servants, with those below them in various roles according to their duty being 2nd Division to 4th Division. The Prime Minister and State Premiers are all in the 1st Division of Pubic Servants, and those Departments below them rank from 2nd Division to 4th Division.

I was to find myself not needing to sit for the Public Service entry examination due to my connections with John Day and my cousin Kay's level three influence within the PMG and the fact that I had the Leaving Certificate. John and Kay had got busy with the necessaries to see my entry on a well-planned red carpet. I was told then by Kay to hightail it down to the third floor of the GPO armed with my Leaving certificate results, a letter of referral from John Day, and one from administration dutifully signed by Kay McPhillips. It took a week to reply that I had 'passed' the entry examination and to be at Customs House at Circular Quay the following Monday at 9 AM to allocate my 3rd Division position. The letter did not stipulate which branch of the Public Service I would be assigned.

Come Monday morning, I arrived at Customs House and was met by a guide. Many graduates of the entry exam were standing with me in the foyer. We were ushered into a large room and asked to be seated. It was like sitting in church waiting for the priest to arrive for the Mass celebration. The duly appointed Public Service spokesman appeared and introduced himself, giving all present a welcome congratulations on acceptance to the Public service. It was much like a Papal blessing followed by communion as he launched into his duties. He briefly explained that there were plenty of jobs to select from any department within the Public Service. He then commenced with the offers, encouraging his department first: "Who wants to join Customs" he said. A show of hands, and then he took down the names. So it followed with the Tax Office, Water Board, PMG, etc.

I had not thought about where I might wish to go, but with my Intermediate-only Maths pass, it could not be the Tax Office. Instead, I opted to stay with the PMG when I raised my hand, and my name was then recorded. Once the names were all written in a book, not unlike what possibly happens when St. Peter enters the chosen ones' names into the Book of Life, we were given a short toilet break, returning to our seats. The duly appointed clerical spokesman raised her head from the lectern and began to call out our names. When it came to me, she said, "Douglas McPhillips, PMG, 2 Primary Works Department, Homebush." I was boarding with a Yugoslavian family in Croydon then, travelling to and from Homebush; my new Class 1 clerical duties above the Homebush post office were a piece of cake, as was the job.

The Master of the house where I was a lodger was Boris of Serbian birthright, and his excellent wife had been of Royal Macedonian bloodline. They were kind people, and their four-bedroom house with three boarders joined together for evening meals proved to be one big happy family. We often discussed how the dutiful wife and cook's family wealth and power went to her male siblings on the death of her father, leaving her and her financially poor husband to migrate to Australia. Without the stories around the family dinner table, I would never have known of the Yugoslavia communist state under Prime Minister Tito; the six republics of Serbia, Croatia, Bosnia and Herzegovina, Macedonia and Montenegro, as well as two provinces of Kosovo and Voivode, combining under the one Federal People's Republic to become known as Yugoslavia. Considering that family fed us and charged minimum boarding cost, we three intrepid lodgers were on a good wicket and learnt much of their history. We learnt of the Austro-Hungarian post-World War 1 hostilities between these Kingdoms which was quelled when Tito came to power. He was the embodiment of what a good Dictator should be, keeping a tight reign on ethnic tensions between the different races of people. This was in the late 1960s, so the pending racial wars of independence for the various republic seats that followed Tito's death decades later were not news.

Boris, who, although not educated like his 'royal' wife, warned of tensions and a bloody future for Yugoslavia. Interestingly, most of what he predicted came to pass as much blood was shed in fighting for independence from the various wars between races. It took until 2006 for independence to reign, for all of the former Yugoslavia regions to be declared independent of one another, for NATO troops to return home and for the UN, EU and USA to recognise the peace that followed a bloody mess.

My daily duties as a clerk in my first official indoctrination to the 3rd Division of the Public Service were the responsibility of all mechanical aids used by the PMG lineman working on the laying of 'Niggerville.'It was a contemptuous term for the possible ethnicity of the pending population to reside there. The suburb's official name is Blacktown. My duties, apart from recording the logistical locations of tractors, trailers, plant and equipment right down to portable toilets, included the pay run once a fortnight. The duties of keeping the officially registered number of all inventory checked and verified every fortnight ensured nothing went astray and could be easily located and moved to another destination at a moment's notice.

The linemen were of white descent, comprising many immigrants as well as white native-born Australians. I can't recall ever seeing a native Aboriginal in the field in the PMG back then. Coming from a country town and growing up with Aboriginal boys as primary school classmates and football buddies, I could not recall ever questioning the colour of their skin, even in those days of the White Australia Policy, as far back as the 1800s, the majority of white Australians shared attitudes towards people of different races that by today's standards were openly racist. Criticisms of non-white groups were based on the idea that they were less advanced morally and intellectually than white men. Australia had focused mainly on people of Asian descent, but this applied equally to all non-whites, including our indigenous population, who were considered a 'dying race.'

All that changed somewhat with immigrants from England and Europe after WWI. Lost souls looking for a new home and way of life. However, even they suffered the slings and arrows of locally born Australian attitudes, being called 'Dago' or 'Spik' as a matter of course. My duties on the fortnightly payday were to meet the Mayne-Neckless 'Money mover' van with three other PMG employees to collect the loot and arrange it for distribution to the linesmen at their particular work locations. The monies were signed over to 'Shorty' the Paymaster, an old grey-haired Senior Clerk who proceeded to haul the load up a two-level staircase with the help of us fellow assignees. It was always a daylight early start, and once we had loot spread across a large table on the top floor of the Homebush Post Office, we counted it all from extensive notes to lesser denominations, sorting the coin in a similar fashion. Once we had ascertained that all the money was there and checked with the payslips, we were each assisted a task in preparing the pay packets for the linesman.

Linesman requested various ways in which they were to receive their wages. Some requested two envelopes, one with the pay slip and cash included in one and another with the overtime and cash for the same included in another envelope. Others still would request a certain sum to be put in a third envelope to pay off their bookie or mistress. Those who chose to spend their overtime on themselves with gambling or drinking sessions or asked for a 'secret fund' envelope could go home with the real wage to their respective wives and hand over what appeared to be their total wage. It was not in our brief to judge but simply to do as asked. This way, we kept the linesman happy and the Unions at bay.

A typical payday would see us on the route in a PMG sedan, with a large battered briefcase of all the pay packets in alphabetical order on the back seat. My job was to ride a shotgun next to the Paymaster with a six-shooter in my jacket pocket. In the passenger front seat, our front-line security guard carried a shotgun on the floor before him. The driver was unarmed but at full alert, being at the wheel. The drill was to drive up beside a group of linesmen on the job, wind down my passenger window, and dish out the pay packets. The linesman would identify who he was, I would call out his name and "Shorty, the Paymaster' would hand over the required number of envelopes to me to give to the wage earner. The next in line would appear at the window, and the procedure would be repeated.

By about 10. am. we would have dispensed with at least half the case of cash pay envelopes. It would then be our morning tea break. We simply drove to the nearest pub or Club, parked the car and locked it with the suitcase left in the back seat. We never worried about the money as it wasn't ours and figured it was insured anyway. We were soon seated at the bar knocking back a few beersrs with our six-shooters hidden and the shotgun down the trouser leg of our front-seater security man. Whilst he should have been on workers' compensation, he preferred light duties and riding shotguns for us instead of being off work. In truth, he did not want the embarrassment of filing a P500 form, although it was the official preliminary form necessary to apply for Workers Comp; in the PMG at the time. My duty was to complete this form to assess his case, but he just would not fill it out. When considering the circumstances of his accident, I could hardly blame him. The accident that ensued, which should have resulted in a time-out for him, was both personally painful and equally embarrassing and if one has a warped sense of humour, somewhat funny.

Our Lineman, whose name shall remain secret to protect his right of anonymity; so as not to cause him any anxiety, was carrying out his daily duties on a given day. Together with another employee, they lifted a manhole lid to climb down into the pit to work on a faulty telephone cable. It had been raining then, and the heavy manhole cover slipped through his hands; he lifted it. This was a bad omen as one corner of the steel lid cut through his pants, slicing his old fellow from top to tip. Our unfortunate hero fell to his knees screaming as blood sprayed every witch way. The fellow worker put down the other end of the steel pit cover he had been holding and ran to a nearby work van extracting a bottle of disinfectant and some bandage from the medical kit. He returned to the scene of personal agony and poured the disinfectant on the treasured body part of our suffering soul. The tortured victim screamed in agony in disbelief at his misfortune. Passersby observed the caring attention of his fellow worker as he wrapped the not-so-small. Still, now dysfunctional weapon with a copious quantity of bandage, winding it around again and again so that our victim would appear to have a tremendous precious gift to be later unwrapped by an enquiring nurse. So the P500 was never completed, so he was riding shotgun on our pay run.

To all intent and purpose, it looked like he had a stiff leg as he hobbled to the bar. I was never quite sure if it was the recovering personal missile that caused his stiffness or the shotgun down his trouser leg. In my case and 'Shorty the Paymaster,' we must have appeared like two gun-toting comical underworld characters from a kid's comic book. Our only other gun-toting duty was every second Thursday we had to adjourn to the rooftop of the GPO in Martin Place for pistol practice. Our duty was to fire six rounds of ammunition with our handguns at a target.

The accuracy of our shooting was never questioned or checked. It was a simple matter of firing the gun as rapidly as possible to get off the six shots, handing the gun back to the duty officer for safekeeping until the next payday and taking off to a nearby bar for a few beers before returning to work. It must be said that, like my school day Marist Brother teachers, I have created nom de plumes for each of the following characters in the happenings of my future career to protect the innocent and not break any of my fellow associate's anonymity. Whilst the facts herein played down are actual, some licence is given for my recall accuracy. Now that I am old, there is always the possibility that my recall is more coloured by my imagination than the workings of my current-day linear conscious mind. So, now read on and weep for those of us who, with the darkness of former deceit, hid the light that every man carries in the depth of his heart.

An opportunity came up a year later through the Government Gazette for a Class 2/3 Clerical promotion with 2 Primary Works stationed at the Carlton Centre in Elizabeth Street City. My duties there and the aftermath of those times still affect telecommunications and city transport. Ron, we shall call him 'the Willing,' to protect his anonymity, was my Divisional Clerk, and I was his dubious 2IC. Ron usually swanned his way into the office around 9.30 a.m., already 30 minutes late for work. This was his daily habit, and mine was not much better. You could always hear him as he entered the nearby corridor singing as he entered his very own tune: " The working class can kiss my ass; I've got a boss's job at last." Ron, not knowing what was on the agenda for the day, always enquired "And what have we as a priority for today sunshine?" Our first official duty together was to proofread a forced retirement package sent from Staff and Industrial for our sign-off on a very generous payout for not-so-old employees on the grounds of ill health. The intended recipient had been a long-term employee of the PMG, a Divisional Clerk in the Engineer-ing Section and a dyed-in-the-wool alcoholic, Joe, whose sur-name shall remain nameless as he has long passed, God rest his soul.

At the time of Joe's pending payout, he was in the depths of alco-holism and was in no way capable of doing his job. Well, at least that is what I was given to understand. Not that it matters much in the case of most Divisional Clerks in the Engineering section of the then PMG and, for that matter, this newly appointed second in charge or as abbreviated 2IC. I had read his personnel file given to me on the quiet by a spy from Staff and Industrial to help me with my decision-making. Joe's daily journey to the city on his way to work was on the Manly ferry; fortunately or unfortunate-ly, it meant passing the 'Ship Inn' public bar. Joe never made it past that bar without first sinking copious amounts of amber fluid to tardy him up for the tasks ahead. Whilst his work-a-day world was limited, it coincidentally proved to be the same for me in the long run with my then-PMG career. However, at the initial ap-pointment, I was a conscious worker and not a conscientious ob-jector, as was later the case with the progressive killing machine of the Vietnam War still in play. I had perused Joe's file and, in my then industrious mind, found it difficult; having given due diligence to the payout for a still suffering alcoholic, I decided not to counter-sign Ron's signature on the document to approve the payout.

The document reappeared at my desk shortly after, and a black biro was handed to me. I looked up, and there hanging over my shoulder was my Divisional Clerk, the Chief Engineer of 2 Primary Works and a Key Personnel Officer from Staff and Industrial. Ron began to speak: "Doug, you have to counter-sign this document. Joe was a Changi prisoner of war who escaped the Japanese after much suffering. He spent fourteen days on a barge in the Pacific Ocean in his escape without food or water and was lucky to make it to allied territory and survive. Without the likes of Joe, neither you nor I would have a job; we, too, would be slaves to the Japanese, so sign the bloody document." I thought of my Toyota car, the Japanese-made radio I owned, and the many Japanese products in my possession, including the biro in my hand, thinking that I was a slave to the Japanese anyway and wondered who had won WW11. I signed away my life on that document and my small reality of noble morals. The task completed all the witnesses to my signature on that retirement package document returned to their dubious tasks. Ron invited me to join him at the New South Wales Leagues Club across the road for a few beers to celebrate Joe's newfound fortune.

Well, as it was 10.30 a.m. and morning tea break, I felt justified to slip away from my apparent duties. It didn't take me long to bury the red tape deed I had just completed. Maybe it was the third, or was it the fifty beer that I realised I had sold my soul to the devil, and Ron had me hooked into more fowl deeds for the future.

So it turned out, that my future dubious document counter-signing approvals were necessary to keep the Government fund allocations rolling, the PMG Engineering work flowing for further job creations, future budget allocations and the topping up of employees' wages too. The usual morning greeting from Ron as he entered the premises continued, "What's on the agenda today, sunshine?" I quickly spelled out the plans and documents for a new Coaxial cable up George Street and further Coaxial cable across the Harbour for the much-needed telephone lines for increasing commercial development in North Sydney.

CHAPTER.6.

HOW TO RUN A PROFITABLE BUSINESS

The typical daily activity was for Ron to adjourn to the bar at the NSW Leagues Club for a few beers on his own with instructions for me to join him after about an hour, having answered a constant ringing of phones. I eventually escaped handing over my duties to the new clerical assistant to keep the ball rolling. What I didn't know was that it was as simple as writing out a list of unanswered enquiries for Ron to complete on his return to the office later in the afternoon. Most of the time, he was on the blower, head down and bum up for the remainder of the day, completing outstanding orders for the Engineers whilst I did most of the paperwork.

Our usual morning ritual together meant I had to leave my desk and head to the Leagues club to join Ron for a schooner or three as a regular daily ritual. Turning up with files of pending Engineering jobs to be perused over copious amounts of alcoholic beverage, we would ascertain how much overtime money each task should be allocated for the Engineering Department, Staff and Industrial, right down to the Technicians and linesmen carrying out their relevant duties, and of course their Clerks and Clerical Assistants. It was considered mandatory and warranted that any job worth its weight for the public's benefit should have an element of overtime monies built into the equation for all and sundry before signing off the approval to go ahead with the work. That was even if the overtime work wasn't warranted or indeed done. So it was that the first of these files of urgency awaited by the Engineers assigned for the task for completion being diligently read and proofed for approval on this fine morning for drinking by my Divisional Clerk and his industrious assistant and fellow drinking mate, 2IC me. It took us two weeks of cross-checking our figures over copious quantities of alcoholic beverages in the Leagues Club to justify the overtime and give our seal of approval. The Head Engineer, Norbert, the Quirky one, was anxiously at my desk day in and day out, waiting for our approval stamp and document signatures. However, Engineers were university-qualified but were answerable to the Administrative staff for all matters, much like the Prime Minister is answerable primarily to the PM department.

We approved 28 hours of overtime for the administration duties of all and sundry for the telephone Coaxial cable to be laid from Circular Quay along George Street to Broadway. The administration could easily have been done in regular working hours, but that would have interfered with good drinking time. So the overtime was approved so that very little was done during the daylight hours. I never felt right about that first Coaxial cable approval and used to go back to the office at night and attempt to do the overtime work. I was the only one in the building after hours; no one did any overtime, and the admin; was drawn out and anatomised over the life of the job.

I soon realised that my efforts were futile and dangerous in a Commonwealth building without approval after lock-up time. So like every other employee, I said naught and accepted the 28 hours of overtime without complaint or completion.

To be fair, however, we did have extra duties that caused us sometimes to stay back after hours without extra pay to sort things out. This, more often than not, was when either the Water Board or the Electricity Commission would call our Office enquiring if we had laid any cable down George Street or some other city local lately. This was the time when no Government Department liaised with another. They simply went ahead with their plans to lay water pipes, electricity and coaxial phone cables without consulting each other and with limited union influence.

The relevant departments never worry too much about sticking to a plan; they just complete their work in an appointed time to justify their extra pay and get on with the next job. All plans, administration records and sundry unofficial overtime had the mark of "completed" and stamped in red. Once done and updated, the files were transported to the basement of the GPO to gather dust in some old filing cabinet or moth-eaten box. There was no archival filing methodology back then. They were simply dumped there and forgotten.

It is interesting to note that when the recent tram rail was in progress for completion up George Street, there were many delays in the contracted Spanish company's completion of the project. The State Government had no plans to verify a broken gas pipe, a telephone cable, or electricity wire cut in the pathway of the rail line being laid. I shrugged when mishaps happened but would protest my innocence of all charges. My job was to approve plans; it was the engineer's duty to see if the plans were followed to the letter and plans filed for future reference by other Governments and other authorities before any future project was approved by either the PMG, Water Authority or Electricity Commission. As those plans could not be found anywhere with the authorities described above, my signature of countersigning approvals was safe in the archives, perhaps in the bowls of the GPO basement. State Government could plead there innocence, having not been informed of what lay beneath the surface of the proposed tramway. It is no wonder that the project took so long to complete, and cost blowouts continued to occur every time a hole hit what was considered a foreign object.

We do not have the history of ancient European artefacts to be considered when digging into the grounds for European essential services and infrastructure. Still, we certainly create our delays without a plan or favour in the underground tangled web of tunnels under the centre of our city and the harbour, for that matter.

The laying of Coaxial cable for both phone and radio frequency was a significant undertaking and continuous work across the waters from a barge on the western side of the Harbour Bridge to the bottom of the harbour and across the North, joining up within pits by linesman on both sides to existing services. There needed to be more administration for us. It was a simple exercise of a supervising Engineer on the barge guiding the bargeman on the roll-out of the cable from an enormous timber reel. The thick round shape of the twisted pair was not Ethernet cable but more likely copper with thousands of strands encased in rubber side by side, making it some 10-15 cm in diameter. As well as rubber and plastic encasement, it was also encased in lead, so the cable itself weighed a Tonne and had to be winched to place at each end for connection. Whilst it was used mainly for linking to satellite antenna facilities, it was also the main electric cable for business connections well before wifi came into being.

 The yellow cable played alongside this Coaxial cable encased in lead and laid under the harbour for telephone connections. If there was a significant blackout on any of the cable networks, the Powers- that didn't fix it- simply laid another cable. So then the link from the North to Eastern Suburbs Harbour tunnel was built, the divers found a spaghetti-like network of coaxial lead-encased pipelines crisscrossing each other. There was no way they could fathom (play on the word) the live cable from the dysfunctional. Once the concrete roadway and the tunnel were completed, the telecommunications Networks were checked. So if anything didn't work, they reverted to the old method of sinking another cable and reconnecting it. Another problem arose continuously for a long time on the Northside. Often when a new copper-filled pipeline was connected throughout the North Sydney area, a significant blackout would occur. This was not poor workmanship but rather persons unknown simply climbing down one street length of pipe undoing the connection, and doing likewise a street away. The disconnected cable was rolled back on a reel, loaded on a truck and driven away. Fortunes were made during those times of cutting away the cable cover to gain a large quantity of copper and lead covering. The problem was solved with the introduction of surveillance cameras.

On the days when I was not drinking at the NSW Leagues Club with Ron, I often made it down the lift to the basement of the Carlton Centre bar at basement level. My assistant junior clerk Barry was always in support; the Carlton Centre Mariner's Bar had a disco-like atmosphere and a modern bar with pretty young barmaid with low-cut blouses showing a plentiful supply of bosom. It attracted the best young men and women after work and the odd alcoholic ones like me during the day. Not only did we relax over a drink or two, but we also got our quick fix of goggle-eyed sexual delight. Returning to the office after no more than a twenty-minute break at the bar, a file in hand giving the impression that we were calling on another department in the building for work purposes, was never questioned. I don't know why we bothered with the file, as no one cared what we did or didn't do in between contract signings.

Before Barry arrived, Kevin filled the job as my junior clerk. He was a teacher from Queensland in Sydney for regular dialysis treatment for his recent kidney transplant. On leave from teaching in Queensland, he was given the job at the PMG as it was close to the hospital for his treatment. Kevin would go down in history as Australia's first successful kidney transplant. Outside of work, we struck up good friendships and regularly met for creative pursuits like making films on Super 8mm and composing music or using a cover song to align with my script and film.

At one time, we had another Ron on relief as our Divisional Clerk whilst Ron "The Willing' was on annual leave. Whilst in attendance, he was assigned a duty for administration. It was a glitch in a plan costing, and he strolled over to my desk, requesting my attention. I explained that as I was busy writing lyrics for a song to pass it on to Kevin. He likewise rejected the request explaining he was busy composing a musical score. Ron, puffing on his pipe, calmly smoking, remarked: "Worse things happen at sea." Kevin and I attended to the matter in our own time, and all was back to normal again for drinking and leisure pursuit times at work.

Apart from the Carlton Centre Marina's Tavern in the basement bar and the NSW Leagues Club over the road in Elizabeth, we had another regular lunchtime drinking hole. It was in nearby Angel Place, commonly known as the Marble Bar. There was another one whose authentic branding did have a Marble bar, but it was not a patch on ours. The bar was a long L-shaped with a thick dark marble top. Entering from the street, it was a quick right turn into a room full of lunchtime drinkers. Occasionally I got sick of the crowds and retreated with a mate from Staff and Industrial to a bar in George Street. It had fond memories for me, as upstairs on level one was where I first got laid. I digress. At that bar, my Staff and Industrial Department friend advised me that I was being spied upon for my excessive drinking.

I did not believe my friend, so he offered to show me my file one evening when no one was there. After work, when the Carlton Centre was empty, we made our way to the third floor of the Staff and Industrial Department for our illegal entry investigation. My drinking companion had a key to the office premises, so entering was no bother as in those days it was before surveillance cameras were introduced for security purposes. My friend in that department pointed to a filing cabinet and instructed me to find my staff detail folder. I read with great interest every detail of my working and private life since joining the P.M.G. Most of it was a glowingly positive report in my favour. However, in the detail, I was now a marked man. A notation of my drinking exploits in my Commonwealth bank days was there, but no mention of my drinking week with Alex, the Russian Engineer, Dangerous Dan, the pilot and the aircraft experiment. Morrie, the former Divisional Clerk for the Head Engineer John Day had certainly done an excellent job hiding that one.

Another of the characters of my time with Primary Works was Wing Fat, a Singaporean-Chinese Engineer. Wing Fat was contracted for three years to the PMG telephone division, and in that short time, he revolutionised the network. He was a genius, but the three-year visa soon ran out, and our Engineering Department, with his administration's help, arranged a Commonwealth grant for a Master's Degree Course at NSW University. The powers that be needed him to attend the course, but it meant another three-year working Visa for Wing Fat.

Between Wing Fat's exploits at winning over many a top Sydney model to join him in bed to complete his congenial sexual desires, he completed a lot of work for the PMG. I doubt if he ever attended the University other than to appear for attendance from time to time. Wing Fat kept a little black book filled with gorgeous-looking women's phone numbers and addresses. He was short and slim, not attractive, but a charm that could win over anyone. His Buddha-like spirit had us all in his tangled web of deception and fun.

On one occasion, he asked me to join him one night on a mission. It was around midnight as we crawled on our stomachs past the Custom Security Office guard station on a Harbour peer. Wing Fat had arranged to meet an illegal ship entering the Harbour under the cover of darkness. At the appointed hour, the small ship docked at the end of the pier, and we climbed on board. I understood that we were there to pick up some bottles of illegal spirits. I drank myself into oblivion whilst Wing Fat disappeared to talk to the Captain for a time. After some hours, with warm-spirited bellies, we crawled past Customs Security as the ship we had been in sailed out of the Harbour once more. I didn't know it then, but Wing Fat had arranged to import a quantity of opium. It all came to light when I was invited to a party at his Vaucluse apartment. Upon arrival, a Chinese doorman stood at the door with quantities of free opium to smoke. I had been his partner in crime, so to speak, and had we been caught on the docks with him carrying the Opium and me just a belly full of whisky, I am sure if we would have said, "Me no understand, speak no English" He would have no doubt left me to attempt to fast talk our way out of it not know the Opium. I can now breathe a sigh of relief that nothing happened other than a hangover in my case.

Inside Wing Fat's den of iniquity, Porn films flicked on the walls whilst half-naked dances moved with rhythmical drum beats and ear-piercing sounds took over my head. I refused the Opium, the drink and the atmosphere. It was nice of Wing Fat to consider me in his party invitation, but it was not my scene. I just didn't like crowds or drug scenes. Somehow I always suspected Wing Fat had an alternate intention of befriending me. He had tried more than once to rope me into his tangled web of illegal activities, but the teaching of the Marist had somehow at least kept such temptations at bay. I owned a little white Triumph Herald with a black leather hardtop back then. I used to park it all day at Police Headquarters with the cop's cars; back then, all their cars were white. So it was not as if I was innocent, but I drew the line in the sand of my moral code and conscious that I could live with.

I parked my car in police HQ for over a year before being approached one day by a diligent Police Inspector with a "Hey, Son, you can't park here; this is for Police cars only." I feigned ignorance, explaining that I had been parking there for an eternity without any Police complaint. I was duly reprimanded and told never to park there again. Not long after that, the parking lot was granted a Security guard. It was a sense of pride in myself that I had been instrumental in creating a job for a deserving soul.

Now that parking became more difficult for me on work days, I approached the Chief Engineer who approved my parking in the PMG vehicle storage lot depot at Woolloomooloo. When Wing Fat got the word that I had scored free parking in the PMG depot, he asked me to arrange to store his car there too. He said he wanted to avoid rocking the boat with the Department Head to permit him. I smelt a rat and soon found the reason for his sly move in getting me to help transport the car to the PMG depot with him. Firstly, the vehicle had never been registered or insured whilst in his possession for the past three years. It was a worn-out piece of junk that was hardly drivable, but Wing Fat continued to drive it from Vaucluse to Woolloomooloo during the week. He always parked it in a different location every day, but irrespective of his selected hideaways, he still managed to cop a parking fine every day. Wing Fat had never paid his parking fines in Australia.

The old car was well known to Chinese students over the years as it was always handed over to the next male student on his arrival in Australia. It simply told the student where to find the car and where the keys were hidden. It was considered a 'not my responsibility' gift from the last University graduate returning to their native homeland or who may have overstayed their visa and had to leave post haste. When Wing Fat and I arrived to pick up the mobile reck in his latest hideaway, there were stacks of unpaid parking tickets under the windscreen wipers, including one for that day and a recent defect notice to say it was being towed away within the next 24 hours.

Wing Fat cleared all the fines, dumped them in a nearby garbage bin, and then removed the tow-away notice sticker from the windscreen. He did not have a licence but insisted I do the talking at the PMG depot to get the car locked away and hidden from view. Once our mutual assignment was completed, we returned to the Domain car park, which was only a stone's throw away from the PMG depot.

The Domain car park with a mobile walkway from the bottom of Woolloomooloo to the nearby Hyde Park Street exit was a short-cut to Elizabeth Street and a quick on-foot commute to our office in the Carlton Centre. I realised back then that it was a better location for me than the previous location with the Police cars at their headquarters. Likewise, it was a safe logistic arrangement for Wing Fat to take shelter "for the car." It was but a short drive to and from his Vaucluse pad. So there was Wing Fat an unlicensed driver behind the wheel of an unregistered and unroadworthy wreck of a car with a stack of parking fines to his credit, riding on a wing and a prayer. Like everything else in his life, Wing Fat was our chance-taking telecommunications genius, gambler, possible drug pusher, ladies' man and a now endorsed reckless driver without any peripheral vision. Shades of Alex the Russian Engineer's driving ability, I had been thinking.

Another of my duties was looking after all the telephone administration for the Eastern Suburbs Telephone Exchanges and line staff working in the pit points between home and the nearest exchange connections. The Eastern Suburbs had different telephone networks in operation for best performance trials. We had the latest in PABX, German technology and the old 'click and clack' systems, which the exchange technicians disagreed with. The new systems had fewer breakdowns and were much easier to resurrect and restore, it was never a significant issue, but I guess they had to have something to complain about. In my travels, I learned all the telephone Exchange codes for ease of access to the buildings; I memorised them in my head, so this knowledge became instrumental in my next career move.

'Tiny', the Clerical Assistant to the Line Inspector, was stationed at Coogee Beach line depot and was quite a character. He took sick leave at one stage and was off for two weeks. I telephoned him on his return to obtain a medical certificate from his GP to ensure his time off was taken from his accumulated sick leave, not his holiday allocation. I inquired about the cause of his illness, and he replied: "Piles for Peers; haemorrhoids for aristocratic assholes." He had a lot of funny saying and often left me in stitches with his antics. Part of my duties included visiting all the line depots with the Line Inspector, who ensured the men were doing their assigned duties. This way, I saw first-hand why we paid the men the extra allowance they received. Their benefits include worker's compensation, accumulative sick leave for each year of service, and holiday pay with a 17.5% leave loading negotiated by the unions. They had concluded an employee would spend more money on holidays than usual. There was also a training levy for new starters and superannuation long before Paul Keating, as Treasure made it compulsory. Again this was to benefit me in my next career move. Like the technicians in the exchange, I learned the whys and wear-fore of the fieldwork. To be fair, I had a good handle on it from my early career on pay duty for the linesman on the Blacktown route.

My next career move came unexpectedly, as good opportunities often do. A workmate from my days in the Commonwealth Bank was now an AMP representative, and he turned up in my office one day to sell me a Life Insurance policy. Stan, the man, had been a work colleague, drinking mate and going to the races together, buddy. In hindsight, although short-lived, my association with him did not do me a great deal of good. My first boss, Mr. Peter, the gatekeeper (every male in the bank in those days was addressed as Mister.) The gatekeeper boss was my first mentor and affectionately called me "McGuarder." I guess he considered me his key support staff member. Mc or Mac in Irish means "Son of support, " so the handle made some sense. Anyhow, Stan, the man was the 2IC of the first branch I worked in for the Bank and was an engaging personality and conscious bank officer, youth worker and fun to be around mate after hours. That is until he later turned to a life of crime.

Stan, the then-insurance salesman, suggested I would be good at selling insurance and offered to introduce me to his Manager. Stan's later exploits surrounding his elicit activities prompted me to herein hide the surname out of respect for his family. So, out of pure curiosity, I agreed to meet his Manager and went to North Sydney to be interviewed by the amiable John Duncan. John had been an ex-Army man and heavyweight champion of Boxing for the military. I liked him from the first meeting, so before I had time to think, I had signed up to represent AMP as an agent. It was the benefits that astounded me; whilst it was a commission-based job and there was no guarantee of future employment, John offered me a guarantee of six months' income almost equal to my then salary plus generous commission based upon each sale, a low rate of interest finance on a new car, a free medical benefits package and after a qualifying period at a low-interest housing loan. So without hesitation, I said a drinking farewell to my old PMG partners in approval of unreal overtime and sundry and thus began a new career in Insurance.

Looking back on it all now, I realise the opportunity of a lifetime I had turned down when the Public Service Board approved me as a Class 5 Clerk with the Prime Minister Department in Canberra. I decided not to take up that post because I was having such a good time in Sydney nightlife back then; what with wine, women and song, why would a young man bother to get serious about job security? Had I taken the job on, in my humble opinion, I would have made my way up the ladder to become Prime Minister or the head of administration.   A few years later in the bush, I had been a State Government Labor Party member, a town delegate for the Country Party, and finally heading the First Secretary job of a new branch of the Liberal Party. In truth, it was not the politics I was interested in but the network of potential clients to be had as I headed for the big smoke once more.

Did you hear no sweeter voices in the music of the bush
Than the roar of trams and buses; and war-whoop of "the push?"
Did the magpies rouse your slumbers with their melodies, sweet and strange?
Did you hear the silver chiming of the bellbirds on the range?
Did perchance, the wild birds' music by your senses was despised,   For
you say you'll stay in Sydney till the bush is civilised.
Would you make it a tea garden and on Sundays have a band,
Where a "bloke" might take his " Sheila" with a "pub" close at hand?
You had better stick to Sydney and make merry with the "Push"
For the bush will never suit you, and you'll never suit the bush.

CHAPTER 7.

BURNT OUT GIZZARDS

Now the next chapter of this book, and indeed the chapters that follow this one, relate to my story that loosely follows real-life events. This writer of tall tales got his inspiration from people, places and incidents that occurred whilst canvassing for Life Insurance Sales in his newly chosen career path. I was not then a writer of fiction as I am now, but a 'Writer on The Rocks' of that well-known Sydney strip in my endeavours to write up an insurance contract to any drinker at the pub that I could persuade over a drink or three to buy a policy. So my client register had academics, pseudo-intellectuals like me, doctors, dentists, public servants, fitters and turners, builders, plumbers and electricians—anyone with 'the look' of a need for a well-planned monitory future. I mainly keep my ear to the barflies who talk about a change in their life, like the birth of a baby, a wedding, kids' education, fear of cash shortages due to the unforeseen and, with time having plenty of money in retirement. The death of someone always sparks up a conversation about the need to cover funeral expenses, leaving those left behind with an adequate income to stay out of the poor house and the taxation benefits that life insurance provides. My client base in the main was mainly through my old contacts in my previous employment.

To be fair, in my first couple of years on the foot and toad, I only wrote enough commission sales to cover my basic financial needs of food, clothing, and shelter. Whilst I was a chain smoker and a relatively heavy drinker, cigarettes and alcohol were very cheap back in the 60s and early 70s and as for gambling, well, I played the pokies infrequently and, whilst following the ponies on Saturday, became a regular pastime, I always limited my day at the races to thirty dollars; giving enough monies to cover my bets and pay for a meat pie with peas and a few beers to boot. More often than not, with the contacts I had in the racing fraternity, I won more often than I lost. Knowing jockeys, trainers, horse knobblier, race fixers and scrappers is far better than trying to pick a winner by studying form.

My real talent back then was spotting an opportunity and closing in on the deal to make a quid. So to return to the basis of these stories herein, the hero's journey is based on happenings of the passing parade of my life with but a few remaining on this earth to confirm my tales. Beyond their roles were yesterday's fare-weather friends of the pubs I frequented and those gangsters of fact that are told as fictitious characters with comical nom de plume names to protect their real identity and to save me from being shot at dawn for truth-telling. So, without any further ado, let me introduce a typical day in the life of this insurance under-writer of those times.

It was a Monday morning in my early life Insurance career when I saw my GP, Doc Watson, at his Macquarie Street practice for my quarterly check-up. It was a timely appointment for in my life, excesses of cigarettes, whisky and wild wild women, and the uncertainty of earning regular income due to the hidden stress-filled nature of the job had increasingly taken its toll. I was suffering from over-the-limit sugar intake from alcohol, with the readings bordering on Type 2 diabetes, and my kidney and liver functions were out of whack. I had the results of my pathology test at hand from three months back, so I was mindful of these readings before entering the surgery of the goodly doctor for my appointment. Doc Watson was none too pleased with my blood test results of the past three months and promptly wrote another referral to the pathology unit to do the test as they were at present. Well, before I could promise Doc Watson that I would do the blood test again before the week was out, he dragged on my arm and wrapped it in a pressure hold with a concerned look on his face, as only an experienced quack can do, watched the mercury on the gadget rise and spoke sternly to me:" Now my fine fellow, your blood pressure is as high as a kite, you must do your bit to improve your lifestyle and take time out to rest."

The method in my madness to sell more insurance policies and thus earn a good living meant that I had to plan by using a neat presentation to win over clientele, all based on an idea I had picked up reading about the success of Ben Franklin. Ben, who sold life Insurance for New York Life, had learnt to sell the sizzle, not the steak, and had a record over twenty-five years in weekly sales of $25,000,000 and never had a blank week. That was enough for me to make a visual of the benefits of life insurance, graphing the help of a policy over a 10, 20, 30 and 40-year period to ensure tax-free monies for the policyholders at critical times in their lifetime. To add icing to the cake, as I made more and more commission, I had enough left over to lay out twenty 100 dollar bills on the first internal page of my visual presentation. My method of selling was simple. I would approach my intended target with an opening statement, presenting the first page of the visual: "This is what I come to talk to you about, money… It comes in bundles of 100; how many do you want?" Then I would get on with the presentation to always be mindful of closing the deal. Whenever a prospect hesitated on the purchase, I would reopen the page, switch the one hundred dollar bills displayed, and comment: "What is it you don't understand."

Then, I would list all the benefits on a sheet of paper down one side of the page, and on the other the premium the potential client needed to pay regularly. I would then tick off each of the benefits, saying: "You get this, and this, and this. etc.; but if you don't do this (pointing to his premium) then you don't get any of the benefits herein (that is when I would put a cross through the lot" On the law of averages, I approached three prospects a day for five days, and sold at least three a week. Sometimes, I would check out Saturday's Sydney Morning Herald for new baby births and knock on the parent's door on Sunday morning to congratulate them on their newborn baby. Usually, I would pick up an extra sale a week out of that effort. On other occasions, I called on homes where.

Of course, who can foresee the future, which sat squat with the spiel I was selling? Looking back now, those regular visits to Doc Watson and the fact that by the time about some six years later, I had given up the cigarettes. I had long ago decided that once the smokes got to " a $1 a pack" I would stop, which I did. Compulsory is no choice as my lungs were being damaged from the nicotine. I note that it costs around $70 per pack for the deadly habit these days. As for the booze, it took another lifetime before I finally gave up the drink, but that's another story.

So back to my visit to Doc Watson on that fine Monday morning. Well, I am standing there out on the street down on George concerned about my blood pressure, and considering that it won't be so hard to avoid too much excitement. That was until I got a tap on their shoulder and who should it be but Dangerous Dan, the crazy pilot from our day as unqualified members of the flying circus, when we were doing aerial strength measurements for the PMG. Well, he twists my arm to join him for breakfast with him at the greasy spoon in the Rocks. Whilst I was a little anxious being with the flying Ace, I was more than ready for bacon and eggs on Turkish followed up with a cup of brewed coffee. So I figured an hour or so with Dan could do no harm.

Dan filled me in on his life since we last parted company back in Dubbo a year earlier. Apparently, Qantas had forgiven him for his crazy stunt that had caused his suspension for a year and he was now a fully-fledged Qantas pilot. The thought ran through my head that Qantas must be desperate for pilots given their 100% safety record and the no plane crashes in their history of flying may soon take a turn for the worst with Dan in the hot seat on International flights. Perhaps I was prejudging the man, as it sounded like he had turned over a new leaf. He tells me he had rented a flat in Maroubra being not too far to travel to the airport at nearby Mascot. And the biggest surprise was that he was now engaged to be married to hostesses he had met on his return to Sydney to get his flying wings. The reality of Dan's craziness was soon to dawn upon me again. We finished breakfast having talked for at least an hour. Dan was feeling thirsty by then and suggested that we stroll through the Suez Canal laneway in The Rocks and make our way to a nearby pub for a farewell drink before parting company. I knew the pub also had an espresso machine so I figured another coffee would do no harm to wash down the food before parting company to get on with my days canvassing; and as Dan was planning to do some window shopping for his beloved before heading home., I felt no danger in staying with him for a bit longer He was on a three-day leave of absence before taking off on his first flight as a pilot from Sydney to London return, I believed all would be fine and dandy to stick around and out of danger.

Well before I had gulped down my coffee with the view to hit the rock and toad, Dan turned the conversation around to my selling Life Insurance and wanted to know more about the benefits of a policy, and if he could qualify to be a candidate for one. He soon had me hooked as he ordered two schooners of beer. It was my policy never to drink in the middle of explaining the benefits of what I then called "the best investment any man could invest good money into," but in Dan's case I made it an exception to my rule. Realising there was no escape I began to take a sip on the beer and before I got to down my third glass Dan had completed and signed the contract. More to the point I had a two-year commission responsibility, meaning I got 70% of the first year's premium upfront as commission and 30% in year two.

Well, Dan wrote a cheque on the spot for two-year premiums, knowing he was covered as soon as I wrote a receipt for his premium contribution. I guess he was also mindful of the death risk he was taking in flying any aircraft, and I saw a sigh of relief cross over his dial as he pocketed the receipt. I was elated of course, as I had earned half a week's wages in that one sale. So now I settled into a heavy drinking session with my new client and presupposed friend.

It was nearly 1 o'clock when two fine feathered friends wandered through the Rocks and down to Circular Quay. We headed for the back room of the Ship Inn to play Kelly pool and got caught up with a couple of fellows that I happened to know from my drinking rounds in the immediate vicinity. So I introduce Dan to 'Slippery Sam' and his sidekick ' Buffalo Bill ' Harris. Sam got his handle 'Slippery' from his many exploits in and around the CDB of Sydney like his forward thinking slipping a spare quid into the breast cavity of a buxom barmaid with the express purpose of taking her home and slipping into bed with her, or slipping some unaware piss pots drink money change on the bar into his own pockets, or slipping a jockey ten quid to fix a race on the coming Saturday by pulling up short in the final furlong. Slippery Sam would bet his last buck on the likely horse who could outpace the one he had fixed with the jockey. He more often than not on the Saturday arvo didn't bother to go to the races but roped in punters in the pub with his bet on the likely winner, not being the favourite that he had arranged with its jockey to slow down in the race; so more often than not he won his wages by deception.

As for Buffalo Harris, well his name was Bill, but he was called 'Buffalo Bill', because he used to be a cattle grazier before he sold up his New England property and headed to the 'Big Smoke' for a change of pace. Now the problem was that in our drinking companions, there were two other Bill Harris.' So to distinguish which Bill we were speaking about we had a handle for each. So 'Seeds' Harris was an agronomist who often joined us in his visits to Sydney from the Bush. His specialty was in the science of seeds for crop production, but he often visited the HQ of companies like Elders Smith and Co. or joined us with a visitor from overseas wishing to find out more about the management of Australian production. Then there was a local Bill Harris who was known as 'Smasher' Harris due to his occupation as a Panel Beater in the car game. So all the conversations with the unrelated Harris' were always distinguished by their handle of Buffalo, Seeds or Smasher; that way there was no mistaken identity if things went right or wrong, especially when some joker came into the bar looking for Bill Harris because he owes him a drink or the monies for a gambling debt, in which the present Buffalo Bill Harris is more like to be the guilty party.

Well, we were all shooting pool taking bets on the winner for quite some time and the drinks continued to flow. Then some bright-eyed and bushy-tailed guy comes sidling up to Slippery Sam wanting to cadge a few bucks out of him, as he reports one of the poker machines at the top of William Street in King's Cross is about to go drop a major jackpot. He reports that this machine has been played all day with not so much as a burp of a cash drip for the players, so it must be about to go. We quickly finished our drinks, and I was relieved to be quitting the Kelly pool at the time as I was just breaking even when we quit and hailed a cab heading to King's Cross.

It must have put a smile on the dial of the Publican to watch four grown drunk men part with sixty dollars each and cash it all into twenty-cent pieces then quickly head to the now vacant machine on the instruction of the joker who wanted to cadge a quid from Slipper Sam. It was agreed that our informant was included in the supposed winnings to be split five ways, but that dam machine took but an hour to eat up all our coin without so much as the sign of a burp or a gurgle. Disappointed but fortified with more alcoholic beverages than we could discern with a sober mind, we headed down Forbes Street to the illegal Casino. It was the most popular of many such gaming rooms in Sydney, reportedly owned by the Kings Cross mafia and a handful of corrupt cops. The signal for entry was three taps on the door a small mail-like window opened and two pairs of eyes appeared to check us out before entry. The place was a hive of activity, with shapely bar-maids with no more than a small bra and skin tights serving drinks, and a canteen providing sausage rolls, meat pies, eggs on toast and tea for those who planned to stay for breakfast. All was served free of charge for gamblers at the roulette, craps and card tables, and those betting on the side. As long as the house got its fair share of the takings, the fun and games continued throughout the night.

It was about this time that a client of mine entered the club and headed straight for the Roulette wheel. Peter the Accountant was a regular at the tables after dreaming up a mathematical formula for winning long before algorithms, artificial intelligence or mobile phone betting became an everyday thing. Peter, placed his bets and for the first twenty minutes, we watched him winning and doubling up on his bets. It was then we followed his patterns and the tables turned against us. So Peter quit playing and cashed in his chips collecting fourteen thousand as a cheque from the teller's window. He was advised by the manager who countersigned the cheque that had he quit twenty minutes beforehand he would be collecting another ten grand on top, for he was that far ahead before we blemished his winning streak. As a non-drinker and happy-go-lucky chap, he said his goodbyes to all and sundry and left the premises fortified with the fat cheque in his wallet.

It was only a couple of weeks after our night on the tiles with my drinking companions that Peter the Accountant phoned me to come see him about buying another Life Insurance policy. He had been back to the Forbes Casino having had another mathematical dream and doubled up winning again, so he wanted to buy another Insurance investment policy. At the time I wrote it, I did the sale like I was with Dangerous Dan, but as Peter was a non-drinker I wrote the contract and receipt for two two-year premiums paid in advance. Once more I was in the money as the saying goes.

Peter the Accountant, flush with cash purchased a new 'E' type Jaguar and headed west to check out an Opal mine on behalf of a client. In evaluating the client's business he was privy to recognising Opals in the raw before they were cut and polished. So a week later he was walking through the opal field at Lightning Ridge and noticed a big rock on the ground, and recognised it as an opal. On his return to Sydney, he had it cut and made into a ring. So another phone call to me and I insured it with an 'All Risk' policy for its wholesale value of $3,000 and pocketed the commission for my efforts. It is said many fear opal is an unlucky stone, and be that true or not, Peters's luck began to change. Firstly he fell over in the bath and smashed the Opal, next whilst driving his 'E' type at high speed he lost control and wrote the car off. Peter escaped without an apparent scratch but the hitch-hiking passengers he had given a lift to hitchhiker not ten minutes before he was killed. Well it seems the reaction to the narrow escape from death for Peter had triggered a blood condition, and Peter was dead within six months. I often related the story of Peter the Accountant's good and bad luck, warning of the dangers of wearing Opal as jewellery decoration.

It was nearly 10 am on the Thursday morning when I farewelled my fine but not-so-well-weathered friends and headed to the pathologist to get my blood test as authorised by Doc Watson the previous Monday. Even though my head was as thick as a brick, my voice sounded like a fog horn and the clothing I had been wearing all week reeked of cigarette smoke; I got through the procedure of blood collection, then went to a public bathroom facility and washed my face, combed my hair, then sprayed my coat and pants with aftershave I carried in my bag, and using toilet paper policed my shoes. I reckoned I was able to lodge the policies I had written to the HQ of the Insurance company and managed to phone up and arrange a couple of appointments for the following Monday, being mindful of my next appointment with Doc Watson on that day. Although worn out and weary from days on the tiles with fellow drinkers and regular losing gamblers, I accepted the invitation from my fellow insurance underwriters and headed to The Rocks and The Royal George Hotel to quench my thirst; fully intent to head home early for a rest and recuperation after a feed at the Brass Rail.

The best-laid plans of mice and men as the saying goes, don't always work to one's advantage. Whilst seated comfortably on a barstool next to a friend of equal standing, that is to say, one who was a chatterbox Insurance man, always on the job, but happiest on the surface with a drink in his hand. It was not long after a drink or three that another couple of insurance men wandered in and pressed the bar for a drink. On seeing me drinking with a like-minded compatriot, a smirk, smile acknowledgment was had, and they moved opposite, leaning against the wall as they scoffed their beers.

An hour or two passed when my companion decided he had to leave as his 'sugar and spice' was waiting at home for him to arrive for the evening meal. I sat drinking there alone, listening to the loudest of the loudmouth Insurance guys putting down another company's Insurance underwriter who was minding his own business nearby.

My blood pressure was in no doubt through the roof by then, and this bloke was annoying me to the point of my Irish nature being incensed by his insults. In truth, if I had not been drinking, in a sober and logical linear state of mind, I would not have adventured further to put my fist in his mouth. He was known as a knockabout boxer of sorts in his spare time and his cousin whom he was drinking with was the then middle-weight champion of amateur ranking in Australia. Jonnie G, the Italian champ was enjoying a break from his training in the company of Hugo G. Well this is where the linear logical half-brain notion of less-than-sober alcoholic sinks even more into the errors of his ways.

CHAPTER 8.

OUT ON THE TILES

In my inebriated state, I politely asked a nearby drinker to remove the stool, contrary to my intentions. As soon as the stool had been moved, I took a calculated leap at the heavyweight non-titled boxer come insurance underwrite; running at him as fast as my legs could carry me, I lifted him with all my might and pinned him beastly against the wall with his feet off the ground. In a sober mind, I never could have managed that. Too soon, his weight got the better of me. As he slipped to his feet again, I pretended that I had let him go on purpose to allow him to regain his balance, duplicated his mouthing off, " If he didn't shut his mouth, I would shut it for him." Well, one thing led to another and the next, we were side by side peeing to our heart's content in adjoining urinals in the pub's lavatory. I was putting on a good front, but sanity prevailed, and I was about to apologise instead of getting into a fistfight I could not win. As luck would have it, Hugo G, the loudmouth B, apologised to me. I shook his hand and left the atmosphere of bad smells, and instead of returning to the bar, I hightailed it back to the street, fully intent on going home. But that was not to be; who should I run slap bang into but Slipper Sam again, ready for another bender.

Well, I remembered what Doc Watson told me about avoiding excitement and getting some rest, but my pleading to Slippery to stop leaning in on my drinking elbow, for I knew there was apt to be more excitement than I wanted to be once more in the company of Slipper. He is on for heading to a card game on the top floor of an illegal gaming den. Furthermore, If I go there, there is every chance that Buffalo Bill or Dangerous Dan could play craps, and I would soon be in a worse pickle than being with Slippery Sam.

Well not being able to say no to the Slippery Sam,   I find myself climbing into a taxi again. Slipper tells the cabby that I was the one flush with the cash and would pay the fare. Considering his generosity on this occasion I dug deep and slipped the cabbie ten quid for his services as we alighted and climbed the fire escape of this old three-story building above a garage. I didn't know it then, but all the cars in that garage had been stolen at some stage by Slippery, and the engine numbers were chiselled to save them from being detected by the authorities. Not that this was likely as I was later privy to the fact that Slippery didn't want to take an Insurance policy with me, as he considered the cars his insurance in an emergency. Besides he had no intention to sell them, instead, he was making a killing now on stolen number plates, so there was no sense in rocking the boat trying to shift the cars anyway.

Entering the den of iniquity I quickly cased the joint to see if Buffalo Bill or Dangerous Dan were in the vicinity. I had no sooner breathed a sigh of relief at their noticeable absence when I was slapped on the shoulder by none other than Hugo G and his bodyguard-middle weight charming cousin. As quick as a flash Hugo ropes me into an idea he has come up with in a light bulb moment since our earlier encounter in the Royal George. He gained my enthusiasm for the fight game and roped me in on being a contender for a boxing match the next night. He figures he will fight Ray, the 'Marlboro Man' in the main bout and I, being a welterweight, he would fix it so I would the support act to fight Sill Furlough, another insurance guy who was weight for age to me, and whom I happen to know as being of British decent and natures gentleman. Hugo G had figured that he would have it all organized for the Saturday evening after the race meeting at Randwick, to be held in a local gym nearby to the track. He just said " You'll have some fun mate, so you will be in it won't you.? We can meet after the races and have a beer and I will give you the lowdown," meaning, the time, and place of the 'exhibition' matches. Well like a mug I agree and find that Hugo is not such a bad egg after all. We part after a few more beers and I had to join Slippery Sam in his craps game. As it was he was I breathed a sigh of relief that I didn't have to cover his bets as he was on a winning streak.

I glanced around the room and found that there was an outside mob around the table; I recognised some. Nick the Greek, my eat-out of choice, of George Street after my usual night on the tiles. Next to him is Big Jim, a giant of a man, wrestler by trade, and Nick's bodyguard, him being another Greek who is paid by Nick in Sirloin steaks for services rendered.

I later note this the next morning when I head to Nick for another feed of bacon and eggs with hash browns and some leftover tomato concoction. Big Jim was I found sitting at the bar well on the way to consuming his third steak when I arrived. He acknowledged me as a friendly guy, and I found out too that Nick was his trainer in wrestling and Sirloin steaks, according to Nick, are the best for an athlete of Big Jim's standing to keep his strength up for matches. Then at the crap table, apart from Slippery Sam, is a guy with a Derby hat on his scone, Harry, the doorman. You know, the guy from the Forbes club whose job is to survey those knocking at the door of the letter box lid peephole and determine if he wants to let them in. He is a truncated servant of the Kings Cross mafia and those reported crooked cops who own the joint. Also around the table is the tipster, Peter the Punter, and Riley, the hit man for the underworld who gets my blood pressure up every time he glances my way. Well, the game goes on until half past five in the morning, and I am dozing in the corner when I get a kick in the ribs from Riley, the hitman, who smiles into my red eyes, saying: " You can always tell the drunkard road racer, he's the one with the bloodshot headlamps." Well, I smile back at him and stagger to the waiting cab with Slippery, Hugo and Jonnie G. waiting for me to climb aboard. We go to Nick, the Greek cafe, who meets us with a warm greeting of "Great day fellows, what will it be?" Nick looks as fresh as a daisy, and I am surprised how he can be so cheerful at that early hour. I found enough time to slip home and have a hot shower and a new set of clothing before heading off to work to prepare my next week's appointment plan.

Day slips into night and old habits die hard as I commence my regular night pub crawl along the strips at the Rocks. Meeting up with some old jazz freaks, I polish off a couple of rounds of cheap red wine and a belly full of meatballs soaked in tomato sauce. I suspect that they were actually dog food dipped in hot tomato sauce, but I have partaken of them many times in the past and not suffered an allergic reaction, so I was not fazed to have my fair share that Friday evening.

Come Saturday, the boys of my company of the week of drinking all gathered at the race track for a pleasant afternoon of gambling and drinking sessions. Surprisingly, I won all the races bar one that Saturday afternoon. It soon gets around the punters that there is a guy who keeps on winning, so the punting Push-on is plucking my brain as to what I will bet on in the second last race of the day. Under pressure, I selected two likely nags, having got the lowdown from an owner-trainer an hour or so before on one nag, and the other I had was a tip in Best Bets. My usual contacts of jockeys, horse stoppers and knobblier were nowhere to be seen that fine afternoon. Pressured by all and sundry who keep saying, "Well, which one will you be on to win?" Once they seemed to be in the know, they abandoned me, and I decided, with some intensity now and blood pressure on high to pick the same horse with little time left to the start of the trace. It ran second by a horse's head to the other one of my selections.

None of the Push bothered me for further tips after that; so I headed for the enclosure only to find an old guy leaning over the fence checking out a nice-looking filly whilst its handler walked it around the enclosure. " You like horses, son?" He enquired. " I quietly responded with mocked enthusiasm: "Yes, Sir!" Then, putting a hand on my shoulder, he whispered closely in my ear, " Horse racing is a mug game, my boy, but as long as you hear, you can put your last dollar on this one; it's my horse, and it will win by at least six lengths today." I thanked my kind owner of the horse and headed for the bookies to place all my hard-won money on this horse. Going against the grain of my usual each-way betting, I put the lot on the nose, and to my surprise, the old guy knew his horse flesh, and it romped home seven lengths ahead of the field as predicted. I never won like that again at a horse meeting, no matter how conservative my betting may have been or any future advice I received. I only wish that I had taken the rest of the old guy's advice: and adhered to the fact that "Punting is a mug's game."

Well, I joined the boys after the races in good spirits and proceeded to drink far too much before the fight intended for later in the evening. Hugo stood up to me giving me the address location for my bout, as well as to all and sundry free invitation to pub patrons to attend the fight. So there was no backing down by me by then. This was to be my only other inherited claim to fame as a boxer. It was a challenge I accepted that I lived to regret. I was unfit at the time, and not in an excellent space to be entering a boxing ring. The guy I fought was the right weight for my age to fight but unknown to me, but undoubtedly known to Hugo, he previously won nine professional fights in England. If I had known that before I stepped into the ring that fight would never have taken place. I of course had no real ring experience, brawled a bit in pubs prior to that fight but that was it, apart from what Uncle John had taught me as a small boy. I managed a draw in that fighting bout out of sheer will, but I know who really won the fight that night.

The very next morning I awoke to swelling all over my face, two black eyes and a cut lip and I felt like I had been hit by a truck. After that experience, I steered clear of fights thereafter, but I did find myself unwittingly in a pub fight or two over the years, more often than not inebriated. Come to think of it I never won in any way as a drinker. I know now, with 20-20 hindsight Hugo certainly set me up for a hiding, but to be fair he did give me a weight for age-equal challenge. In retrospect, it would have been better to have apologised to Hugo for my angry actions in the first instance and I would not have been walking around in a daze for twenty-four hours after the event.

Returning home to find Slippery Sam seated in the back seat of an auto with his driver 'Hop-In' Harry at the wheel. Well we're back in the club over Slippery's garage, and there's no room at the crap table, so Slippery lets out an " SH one T fellows" and pretty soon there is space at the table for Slippery and me too. Slippery notices the sallow face stick of a man with the Derby hat from a Friday night game is about to throw dice, and he says to him: "Who is the spinner here?" and right then and there the weedy bloke says:" Why you are Slippery" and hands him the dice, and out of respect his Derby.

 Nobody pays much attention to me, perhaps figuring that after my fight the previous night I wasn't there to cause trouble. Well, Slippery rolls the dice around and throws them into the hat declaring "Ten" without so much as any-one being game to look inside the Derby hat, other than Slippery to see if his call is accurate, and no one is going to catchSlippery Sam cheating or call him a lier to his face. Well, the game plays on, and Slippery seems to be having loads of luck, when suddenly he quits, grabs a bunch of notes declaring"This is enough for me tonight" from his supposed ill-gotten gains and leaves a goodly percentage for the punters left behind who are most grateful to Slippery Sam for his kindness. He hands the Derby hat back to the weedy bloke and motions his hand to me to come on.

Well, the palace had got all silent and it began to give me the creeps and raise my blood pressure up a notch or two. Someone calls us as we left the Club; "Slippery you sure do make your dough the hard way." There is a fit of laughter from the rabble at the craps table. I never knew if Slippery won his bets legitimately with those dice in the Derby and no one else was privy to that either. Well, I am about ready to go home but Slippery gains disappointed at this suggestion; saying: " Stay with me cause I like your company."

Well at that point I was feeling a bit crook and my head still pounding, and save for the dark glasses to hide my shiners, I was looking rather sickly and grim. I remembered Doc Watson insisting that I needed to get more sleep for the sake of my health, but Slippery Sam would have none of it. He's on for kicking on dancing to the beat of his own drum, and he insists he is in need of my ear to listen to his moaning and groaning about the state of the economy and somewhat and such and such and how he planned to fix it all. So I see it is no use arguing with Slippery or hurting his feelings, so we head downtown to The Horse and Thistle hotel with the jockey who is driving the cab, and he's driving so fast I'm praying for him to slow down and my blood pressure is rising, but he is deeply in conversation with Slippery and neither takes a scrap of notice of the speed or acknowledge my concern. I tried leaning over the driver's left shoulder and shouted in his ear to please slow down, but he ignored me and kept busting along. Next thing I know, Slippery insists the jockey stops the cab.

Slippery stands on the street with his head leaning in the car and says: "When your customer who is paying your cab fare tells you to slow up, you should oblige and take it easy." Well, I am relieved and at the same time surprised as I wasn't aware that it was my duty to pay the driver. Next thing Slippery grabs the jockey and drags him through the passenger door slaps him around and pins a punch on his chin. So before I can say 'Jack Robinson,' the jockey is running up the street to escape leaving Slippery Sam and me stranded with the cab. Well as quick as a flash Slippery is behind the wheel leaving me on the curb and he's after the bloke. I hear a 'woolly ' and by the time I arrive on the scene, the poor guy is lying flat out cold on the ground. So Slippery motions that I get back in the cab and he leaves the guy still out cold. There is one thing Slippery Sam doesn't want is to be answering to the cops. He pulls up a block away from the Horse and Thistle with the view that someone will find the abandoned cab and turn it into the cab company. No sooner do we step out of the cab, than a cop in uniform comes waltzing up declaring that we can't park there. Well, knowing Slippery Sam he is not one for taking advice, especially from a copper. So he takes a peek about to make sure nobody is a witness and he king hits the copper knocking him to kingdom come. Now we have a cab jockey and a cop laying flat in a coma not more than a street apart from each other. Well before the copper hits the sidewalk Slippery grabs me by the arm and starts us running away, so we dash into the 'Horse and Thistle' to join the crowd of responsible citizens from the nearby neighbourhood playing cards and cracking jokes. Nobody gives Slippery Sam the time of day, but for once I am sure he was glad of that. We leave the pub after a few quiet beers and check the street. There is no cop to be seen and the can is globe too. We hail another cab, and here I am hoping that Slippery Sam keeps his cool and doesn't hit this jockey driver too. So I gladly volunteered to pay the cab fare seeing I didn't have to pay the last one.

Well, it's coming up daylight when Sam insists we head for Charley Club for a refresher beer or two to drink ourselves sober. Surprisingly the Club is still in full swing with some customers dressed like they have been to a PJs party and haven't yet been home to change for work. Likewise, there are some well-dressed gentlemen and ladies obviously having enjoyed the night at a wedding or Elite function, and some not so well to do, in fact, the worst for wear having a recovery drink to finish off what they probably consider is left of the weekend. Slippery has Charley Chan stake him for a few quid to play the pokies and once more he 'soon is on a losing streak. When the money is all gone he tells Charley he will pay him back next week, but his good intentions always leave Charley all the more poorer for knowing Slippery.

Well, we're on the street once more and Slippery Sam invites me home for breakfast, as he lives but two blocks from Charley Chan's Clubhouse. I tell him I have appointments and need to go home, clean up, and get into work clobber, but he will have none of it " My Missus will make us both some bacon and eggs mate, so let's finish the weekend on a good note." He says. Well on the way to his pad, he lets me in on some information that he's deep in debt to the wrong types who double the interest bill every day it's outstanding, and they are the types that will come gunning for him, literally. He tells me with a glimmer of sadness in his eyes that it seems he may have to sell the cars hidden in his garage, Even though they were his security blanket for retirement, he articulated with sound reasoning that it's more important to pay out the loan sharks than worry about his ultimate retirement for he fears he won't make retirement if he doesn't pay up soon. We climb the stairs to Slippery Sam's flat and without so much as a how do you do, tell his slipper of a Dolly Bird to "Slap on some bacon and eggs for me and my friend here." So that little blond bombshell of a thing, half Slippery's height, swings back her fists and punches Slippery fair on the nose. Then with one might push he lands on the lounge chair set up behind him. "Oh! Come on Doll " he pleads. Then she turns on me. " So you're the bastard who has been leading my man astray all weekend you bastard" For a moment she hesitates and returns to the kitchen. I can hear the pots and pans rattling and figure she is going to cook us bacon and eggs after all, but I am mistaken. Dolly bird, whose name I never knew because Slippery didn't introduce us, comes racing at me with the frying pan. I now figure it's time to hightail it out of there and head for the door to the stairway exit. Then the next thing I know, a great explosion goes off in my head as this blond bombshell clunks me over the head. Well, I'm dazed but wiser for the leaving, for I can hear her yelling for all its worth at Slippery Sam as I make it to the street: " I cooked you this baked dinner last night and you don't even have the courtesy to come home and eat it with me." It is apparent Dolly Bird has thrown the meal at Slippery Sam for I could hear him say" Err, Gee Doll face, I'm sorry." "Sorry are you, well I know you like your potatoes mashed so here you are. " I imagine she is jumping up and down with the potatoes under her feet. There you are, they are mashed now."

It's 8.45 a.m. as I make my way to Doc Watson's surgery for my medical appointment as planned the previous week. I made sure I left my sunglasses on to hide my black eyes, as Doc Watson greets me. So I first tell him about my headache and he produces a couple of dissolvable aspirin and a glass of water without so much as a how do you do. Then he checked my blood pressure and proceeded to read the results of the blood test I had on a Wednesday: " Well son, all your vitals are back to normal, and so is your blood pressure, and I declare you are in perfect health and have nothing to worry about." Then I hear as I head for the door: "It just goes to show what a little bit of rest and quiet living will do for your health."

The cobblestoned streets of Playfair and Atherden have always held much character that is what is called the Rocks Square boarding George Street near what is known as Circular Quay. The walls of the buildings along Atrheden still resemble those of my drinking days being of concrete and stone in the main, save for one wall made of hardwood timber. What is unique about this particular wall is that it has a doorway inconspicuously hidden to the naked eye about halfway along the fence which, if you were none the wiser you would miss it. Those who are privy to this doorway know that what lies behind it is a bar room, a kitchen and an eatery. It is those of gangster mentality that frequent the place. Others who are invited like cops on the take, undesirables on the run from the law or other rival enemies, and of course the innocents who just like the atmosphere of rubbing shoulders with the elite of crime and punishment.

CHAPTER 9.

HERO OF INIQUITY

As a drinker of no certain talent, I was invited on more than one occasion, by the worst and the best of humanity, to be a part of the action of " The Den" as it was known, never sure of what that action might be. I didn't care much for the company I kept there either, as long as I had a drink in my hand I was content to be there. Apart from the inventory of a good supply of cheap liquor being always on hand, the joint had the best of the day catch supplied from the Sydney Fish Markets every Friday. This evening was no exception as I remained seated in the eatery awaiting my dinner of Ocean Trout caught that very morning. Fortified by the best of beer I watched the parade of Lawyers so-liciting fee advise over drinks to some definite gangster who was to be charged with murdering an underworld figure earlier in the week. Making up the best of a bad lot was a half dozen heavies there to protect the shooter from any potential dangers from ri-vals. I happened to be invited by a Loss Assessor whose income was mainly derived from filming victims on Worker's Compensa-tion who were deriving income from often non-existent back in-juries. I found out later that he was keen to get me to join him in his employ on a salary as opposed to my uncertain commission-based earnings which then derived my living. So there I was seat-ed partaking in the best of fish and chips and sipping on a cool beer awaiting my pre-arranged appointment with the man who has it in mind for me to be a "Peeping Tom" in film making for the Insurance company. A nondescript filmmaker peeping on shonky claimants to catch them in the act of doing something that contravenes the Insurance Act.

Whilst I am busy on my form guide and checking out who comes and goes in the place; in steps a stranger and sit down at my table. I paid little attention to him at first, for I was too busy evaluating potential winners for the next day's horse racing. I hear the strange little man tell the waiter to bring him some fish and chips, too. Well, it takes less than a couple of minutes and the guy starts crying over his meals and beer about a bust-up with his girlfriend. It is something I am not qualified to get involved in, for in my view on such an occasion it is best to steer clear of his troubles and can see that he just wants to unload. So I allow him to rattle on and every now and again I gaze over the top of my newspaper and nod as if I am listening to the pain within his broken heart. It is then I am saved from this dumper of bad tidings as Possum arrives and plonks himself in the corner of the bar that he calls his own.

It is to be noted on the corner wall above his head is a small plaque that has engraved on it "Possums Corner." It was palace there by a Barrister friend of his who regularly drinks with the man of great wisdom. You have to know the Possum to understand why he has that handle. It's the fact that he stands little more than two hands to a grasshopper tall, weighing no more than a jug of beer, with a whisk hair above his top lip he calls his moustache, wetting it by running his tongue over the surface of hair every couple of minutes to keep it looking moist. The Possum has dark thick eyebrows below a permanent frown on his narrow brow, his sad brown eyes appear to be focused on his drinking company in every word and his bowling bald head he always hides under an old straw hat. More so is the man's qualifications which he used with much discernment and the appearance of wisdom. Possum works for the Solicitor General's Department as a clerical assistant in Class 1 of the lowest order, but his great skill is his listening ability or the appearance of such. So much so that the majority of barristers, lawyers and judges are his drinking companions and mouth off to the Possum who never so much as cracks a lay on any subject matter, yet those who employ his services seem to leave his company having drawn greater wisdom of their own making. Incidentally, I do not know the Possums real name, and does seem anyone else does either.

Well, the little stranger still; crying in his battered fish and beer is slow to tell his tale of woe. So I take the opportunity When he poises in his wailing to take a deep breath, to introduce him to the Possum, in the pure intent and uncertain hope that he gains some emotional encouragement from our learned employee of the Solicitor Generals Department. Suffice it to say that the stranger,. apart from having no moustache or hat, appears to be like a twin version of the Possum himself. Although his taste in clothing is somewhat different too, for he is wearing a suit the colour of a baby's poo with a similar coloured shirt of hash brown and a country-wide matching brown tie. The Possum on the other hand is in his usual dark grey suit with a white shirt and pin-stripe black tie. As for the shoe leather, they both are wearing brown brogues. Well, it's not too long before the stranger, who ultimately introduces himself as Tom McSweet, is deep in conversation with Possum when all are interrupted by the heavy knock on the front door by a new batch of coppers and the leading voice crying out " Open up in the name of the law." This is enough to have the coppers on the take bolt out of the place via the fire escape. Just in time it seems for the keen new team wishing to show their effectiveness produced a warrant and handed it to the manager behind the bar, with a copy for the cook and sundry to consider. " Now we do not want any trouble from youse." says burly

Lieutenant McFergus. "So everybody stands facing the wall while we frisk you for illegal weapons." In truth, they are after Angelo the Italian who lives around Kings Cross and he informs the patrons of the Den that he is suspected of being involved in a recent bank robbery. " Now don't go trying outback to the fire escape" says the burly lieutenant:: "We have that covered too," he says altogether too late.

As it happens Angelo the Italian tells it later how he and his associate "Handy Charlie" held up the E.S & A Bank in the heart of the Cross earlier that day. They had a hearse as the getaway vehicle that they had stolen outside the funeral parlour to do the job. The local cops were quick to chase the getaway robbers down Williams Street, Kings Cross, and as they took a right-hand turn to head north over the Harbour bridge the back door flew open and outshot a coffin with a body in it. The casket went sliding down William Street much to the surprise of the bank robbers, cops and passing pedestrians. It was enough of a distraction for Angleo and his Mafia bank bandits to dump the hearse in a car park and hightail it to the underground rail network at Town Hall station boarding a train to Wynyard. Now here they are settled in the den of thieves with their minders when the cops arrive. The quick brain of Angelo had the chief cook and bottle washer hide the loot inside the chook prepared for lunch and blocked the rear passage of the tasty dish with bread and herb stuffing to hide the ill-gotten goods.

So here was Angelo in the company of his Mafia bank robber assistant " Handy Charlie," who was always available to assist Angelo, drinking Italian wine with two other dregs of the social class, Irish Joe, and Big Jim the Greek, the heavy minder for Nick the Greek who is also present but aloof, just watching the goings on in the Den whilst discussing the likely winner of the main event at the boxing stadium with Irish Pat the teller of his many exploits. Pat was known to be always a year or two ahead of anyone including the boxing coaches or horse trainer when it came to picking winners. Nick the Greek listened intently to the Irish tipster just s the cops began their frisking for weapons of mass destruction. The new breed of coppers frisking the mob and the "Rank and File' boss of the Waterside Workers union for good measure. The cops frisk all the suspects and sundry they considered might be in on the crime of the morning's bank robbery including the innocent barfly Possum. The Lieutenant scratched his head with wonder as to the fact that not one gun was found on the suspects, the bad eggs, the dirty dozen or so including sundry innocents.

Anyhow, the coppers are very disgusted with their frisking, not finding any shooting irons or knives, and the barmen, Angelo and Nick the Greek all pipe up in unison saying they are going to contact the Chief of Police and the city Mayor to find out if law-abiding citizens can be stood up and frisks for shooting irons. Lieutenant Mc Fergus is all apologetic now: " Well," he says, " I guess we were on a bum steer, but I bet you a bottom dollar the guns are hidden here somewhere." He follows up with:" We'd be doing a further search here for good measure."

It seems on further inspection that nothing is suspicious. Knowing the Possum is friendly with the Police Commissioner, and the Push of the Rocks, Barristers and Lawyers of this fair city they leave him alone, not bothering to frisk him. The coppers had overlooked the small pale face creature crying innocently with The Possum consoling him. The wise old Possum has much life experience and advises the innocent Tom McSweet to "sit perfectly still and mind your own business, for these toting guns will be in deep trouble with this new breed of coppers."

The coppers are about to leave the Den of Thieves, when little Tom, after spilling his guts on his loved lost state of beings to the Possum, takes a hankie from his coat pocket, accidentally pulls a small pistol unknowingly from his pocket, and greatly surprises drops it to the floor. Tom McSweet does exactly as he is told for in their haste the coppers like a team of players in a maul in a Rugby match pin the poor creature to the wall and begin to frisk him. To the great surprise of the McFergus and his new breed of coppers, Tom has an arsenal of guns on his personage. Twelve pistols in all, two knives and a semi-automatic Tommy gun.

So the next thing we know is the headlines in the Sydney Morning Herald: "Twelve Gun Tommy arrested for carrying unlicensed pistols." The Judge is sceptical of the whole episode, as he has heard all about it from The Possum before he entered the court. It is of course Possum's version which doesn't ring true to form but, nonetheless, it's accurate enough in Possum's eyes for the Judge to show lenience to the accused.

The real facts however are what The Possum told me over a few beers before he told the Judge the version he needed to know. The fact is as the Possum told me:" When the coppers shouted on arrival at the Den door, 'Open in the name of the Law,' the barman, the cook, Angelo the Italian and his sidekick ' Handy Charlie, all rush around the patrons of the Den of thieves and collect all the guns then tossed them into a sugar bag and sat them on the lap of the Possum. In the confusion that follows as the coppers frisk all bar Tom McSweet, the Possum lays one hand on his new acquaintance's shoulder to console him, whilst loading his waistcoat and trousers with all the weapons of mass destruction.

So standing before the Judge now Lieutenant McFergus says that he could tell by the way he acted that twelve-gun Tommy is undoubtedly an almighty killer whom he suspects also of being the culprit who stole the hearse at Kings Cross and drove it as the getaway vehicle in the robbery of the E.S & A bank on the previous Friday. The story gets bogged down in muddy assumptions by McFergus, accusing without proof, Angelo the Italian and his sidekick of the crime of theft of a body in the coffin under false pretences and suspicion of bank robbery.

The Judge brings down his Gavel hard on the bench and Tommy stands in the dock and almost pees his pants, shaking even more than he did when first arrested. In time however, as the case continues and other witnesses including the cook, who still has not cooked the chook that holds the loot from the robbery in the fridge of the Den of Thieves, give their version of events, Tom seems to be gaining some composure, realising that all the attention is about him and decides he will probably plead guilty, for he has noticed the love of his life, who guilted him not forty-eight hours before, is in the courtroom listening to the evidence against her not so long lost betrothed. The courtroom balcony seats are swelling now with citizens of the Rocks eager to see a desperate enough character Tom McSweet accused of carrying twelve guns, and among them are some ladies of the night pushing and shoving their way to the front of the crowded courtroom in hope that maybe when the law allows to take photos that they can be in the snapshots with the accused, now being called by most as 'Twelve gun Tommy'. Soon to have as his handle "Tommy Gunn."

Tom the innocent weak-kneed little fellow has already made up his mind that should he be released from this nightmare he will change his name from Thomas McSweet to ' Tommy Gunn,' for he likes the association with being a tough gunslinger and begins to gain confidence, but soon loses it again when the Judge suddenly bellows, after sizing the accused Tom McSweet over his spectacles, in a loud voice to Lieutenant Mc Fergus: ' Now see here 'lieu-ten-ant', are you telling this court that this half point here is the desperate Twelve-Gun Tommy that you've captured from an illegal establishment that, for the record of the court, is a private meeting place for law-abiding citizens, members of the press and the law?'

It is now dawning on McFergus that the Judge may come down on him with the wrath of God's law,' so he quickly gathers the guns from around the courtroom from his new breed of coppers that were taken from the scene of the crime, and lays them across the bench, claiming them all as exhibit 'A,' pronounces: 'The guns were all taken from Tom McSweet at the Den of Thieves," to which the judge replies: "there is no such establishment in the Rocks known as 'the Den of Thieves,' as I have pointed out before, it is a private establishment for citizens and the law as guests of the owners.

In the wisdom of the Judge, he instructs the now and again shaking Tom McSweet to stand up before the bench where he can get a closer look at him. The Judge then instructs McFergus to plant two guns in each of the side pockets of Tommy's jacket, two in his hip pockets, one in each side of his waist belt and the rest he loads in Tommy's waistcoat. The little man begins to sink to his knee with the weight of the pistols on his personage. The good Judge asks him to step closer to the bench saying: "I wish to see for myself what kind of gangster you are."

Well, as Tommie takes one step forward he topples over and knocks himself out as a consequence of his action. The Judge then discerns that he is naturally top-heavy from the shooting irons. As he falls Tommy's renewed love of his life, quickly runs forward and falls to her knees holding his head in her lap crying out: " Darling forgive me. I love you," Tommy Gunn, in his new persona, opens one eye and smiles at his girl, forgetting all the pain she has caused him and the fact that he wouldn't be before the judge in current circumstances if she had not walked out on him in the first place. Dolly Bird knows in her heart of hearts that Tommy Gunn is the one for he has grown to be the greatest gun-man of them all in just one night. " He whispers to her "I Love you too." And this Dolly Bird says: "Oh, never realised what a hero you are until I read this morning's paper."

Now the Judge is watching all the goings on, but he has already made up his mind, partly based on the evidence of the Possum earlier in the day and partly what he had just witnessed. Tommy finally gets on his feet and the Judge takes him into his private quarters for a QT chat after McFergus relieves him of the weight of the shooting irons on the judge's instructions.

The judge returns to the court declaring Tommy innocent of any crime except lovesickness, and together with his Dolly Bird, Tommy McSweet walks out of Court arm in arm with the love of his life. Now content and wiser for the experience he heads to the registry office of Birth, Deaths and Marriages to firstly change his name to Tommy Gunn and to apply for a marriage licence.

Well, it seems that Tommy Gunn is offered a job as a licensed Gun dealer in the Cross but opts out over time for a career choice in favour of joining the Police force after he marries Dolly Bird. For a guy with such a desperate reputation, Tommy Gunn is bound to make wrongdoers do the right thing. And besides he has a might to land not-so-criminal characters before the Judge, who gains his living and reputation of goodwill to his fellow man by proclaiming all and sundry innocent of all charges. And besides, Tommy Gunn as a Constable has Darlinghurst, King's Cross and the Rocks as his beat. These days he is often seen, when off duty, with Angelo the Italian and the citizens of the Den of Thieves on a Friday night, and of course his old pal in the corner of the bar seated under a sign that says: "Possum's Corner," And as far as the Push of The Rocks is concerned he will always be Tommy Gunn, a one time carrier of concealed weapons for the heavies.

 I was thinking of a particular night of drinking at The Rocks and recall how I had parked my car in the old PMG Dept at Wool-loomooloo, which my former employer had no issue with me do-ing. After all, I was the provider of financial security for the tech-nicians and line staff for the CDB and Eastern Suburbs in my new role of Insurance Representative.

Somehow, I had collected my car in a not-too-sober state and was driving through the back of Kings Cross on my way home. I still had that instinct that my father had taught me of listening to the motor when changing gears, But the steering seemed so heavy at the time that I decided to check the tyres. Sure enough, I had a flat. So, up to the challenge, despite my drunkard state, I managed to get the spare tyre out of the boot, jack the wheel up, and change the tyre. Well, that is what I thought I had done. I tightened the nuts on the wheel, put away the jack, and the assumed flat tyre. I was rather proud of my ability despite being unsteady and drove home. As I pulled into the driveway, I had the presence of mind to recheck the tyre; sure enough, it was flat. In all my supreme effort to change the tyre, I had put the flat one back on the car. Just goes to show how stupid a drunk driver can be.

The following chapter will endorse the skill and stupidity of a not-often-sober driver of my youth. Now read **on**

CHAPTER 10.

CRAZY CAPERS IN CARS

To get a handle on the crazy character that I was as a young man behind the wheel of any car, we have to go back a generation to see where I inherited my DNA from, and how it impacted my devil-may-care attitude when behind the wheel, or more particularly whilst driving under the influence. I could blame my father for his teaching me the tricks of the trade in motoring, but it really was me at the heart of it in truth. It is worth some consideration to look into the kink in my Dad that produced my crazy capers behind the wheel.

Dad joined Clive Sayer's Engineering business in Macksville in 1943 and I was born a year later. He often told of his early exploits as the junior mechanic working for Clive. The one that come to mind as the most interesting was when the whole staff except the most junior mechanics, of which Dad was one, were invited to a local business Christmas party. Dad was peeved about it and decided with one of his mechanic mates to make the party attendees pay for their indiscretion. He took along another mate, Mick Denham as 'cockatoo,' a lookout for his pending prank. All three had made their way to the home of the businessman where the party was in progress. It was agreed that Mick would jump the back fence and check that there was no one who could identify the two young mechanics when they went into prank mode.

As fate would have it, Mick jumped the fence and who should be on the other side but a vicious German shepherd guard dog. Mick had primed himself with enough alcohol prior to this endeavour to have no fear of the consequences and immediately dropped to the ground on all fours and advanced towards the approaching growling dog. The two met face to face in a split second and Mick out-growled the savage beast. The dog backed off and Mick kept advancing towards the animal, still on all fours and barking wildly. Eventually, the dog got the message and headed for its kennel. Mick then cased the back and front yards of the house before returning to the pranksters in readiness to give the all-clear.

 The cars of the mid-1940s were open without locking devices with wind-up windows or canvass see-through side windscreens, so it was not an issue for the two young mechanics to set each car up for the prank. The cars had manual gear sticks back then and the handbrake was the only other safety feature that had to be let off by metal squeezing a trigger-like handle in order to put the car into drive mode. The two pranksters wired the metal handle to the battery so that when the car started the driver would get an electric shock. After setting each car belonging to the partygoers in this fashion, they returned to the next task. They took the wheel jacks from each of the cars and put a jack under the axle of each car so that the back wheels were slightly off the ground but undetectable to the naked eye.

They had only just completed their endeavour when the first of the car owners returned to his car. He started his motor and attempted to release the handbrake at the same time letting out an almighty scream. He swore and tried to reverse the car but the wheels just spun and he was stuck. He returned inside to tell his fellow partygoers what had happened. In a matter of minutes, all the drivers were trying to figure out how to get the car moving and many in their own cars fell for the trap of attempting to let the handbrake off after starting the motor. Vehicle wheels were left spinning but the cars remained stationary and had perplexed drivers scratching their heads. It was a cloudy night and primed with alcohol they elected to return in the morning to retrieve their cars. Dad and his two companions sat hidden from view behind a nearby fence watching the proceedings and had trouble containing their laughter. Clive Sayer related the story about his car the next day to all and sundry but was none the wiser that it was Dad and his fellow employee who had done the ghastly deeds. The secret remained for the life of Dad's career with Clive Sayer and ultimately he purchased the business from Clive when he retired.

Another incident I recall as a young teenager on holidays, was when I managed to travel with Dad and a group of athletes to the professional running Gift event at Dorrigo. There was always a load of prize money to be won at these Gift carnivals as they were professional events. Dad drove his utility with Trevor Owens who was appointed to use a sawn-off shotgun to start races in preference to a starter pistol. So Trevor and his sidekick shotgun ventured up the Dorrigo mountain via the Waterfall Way for the events in the company of local athletes. We left home before sunrise travelling in the utility in the back of which a number of hopeful sprinters and skilled rugby league footballs lay under blanks to keep warm for it was an Autumn morning and quite chilly. As we crossed the low bridge below the Dorrigo mountain, Trevor, encouraged by Dad, put the shotgun out the window, pointed it skyward as he traditionally had done for starting races, and let go of both barrels. The noise echoed through the valley and the half-asleep runners in the back almost shit themselves. Both Trevor and Dad could not stop laughing.

My introduction to being behind the wheel started before I was a teenager. My cousin was visiting from afar and had arrived in his VW Beetle. He was still asleep when I snuck out with his keys and proceeded to start the car and drive it down the laneway behind the family home. Cousin Max had heard the car start and as quick as a flash he was at the side of the car before I got up to speed. In my teens, Dad taught me a thing or two about looking after motors and driving. The first act was to pull down a gearbox and spread it out across the garage floor explaining how each cog in the thing intertwined into the correct position when the driver engaged the foot pedals to change gears. There were no synchromesh gearboxes back then, so the driver had to hold on to the clutch with the left foot to engage the gears before pressing down on the accelerator with the right foot.

I learnt to drive in a WW11 Blitz wagon which made the task even more difficult to change gears; for it meant double shuffling the left foot to get the cogs aligned in the gearbox before acceleration using the right foot. Well to Dad's credit, he made me practice driving that military vehicle around and around the Showground until I mastered the skill of driving the tank. Then as soon as I got my driving permit at age 16, Dad delegated to me the task of collecting a brand new International Harvester tractor from the goods train at the local station sent from Sydney after landing by ship from America.

No doubt, Dad delegating the responsibility to me to drive that tractor helped boost my confidence as an on-the-road driver. So before I returned to boarding school at the end of the holidays I had my driving licence. It was a relatively easy task. The local Sergeant of Police had me drive him around the town whilst he made his rounds to do his banking, post the mail and collect his groceries. Then I drove him back to the Police station a mile away on the edge of town, answered a couple of questions on the road rules and he promptly issued me with my driver's license. I was only seventeen, but rearing to go, for my hero was James Dean and I could hardly wait to return for the next school holidays to play 'chicken' in a car.

Up to that time we kids played that dangerous game on push bikes. We were mirroring the movie 'Rebel Without a Cause' Jim Stark (James Dean) and John 'Plato' Crawford (Sal Mineo) played a game of chicken, racing headlong towards a cliff. In the chicken game, drivers jump out of the cars just before they go over the cliff. The first to jump out was nominated as 'Chicken.' 'Plato' dies when his coat sleeve gets caught in the door handle of his car and he goes over the cliff, Jim Stark (Dean) jumps out in time and is tagged with being 'Chicken.' The troubled teenage youth of James Dean in this movie and in all his performances made him a hero to look up to for us equally troubled youth of the 1950s. Tragically Dean died in a car crash driving his racing Porsche which he named the 'Little bastard' and had it painted under the car's emblem. He was killed instantly along with his passenger in Cholame, California September 1955. However, the passion of my youth overlooked the danger, for like licensed mates I wanted to do a 'chicken run ' as soon as I returned home from boarding school in the Christmas holidays.

Well, my first attack of the crazies in a car didn't start with the chicken run. I had the pleasure of drinking 'Shandies' with my father and his mates one mid-Sunday morning. Incidentally, if you don't know what a 'Shandie' is, it's a large beer with half lemonade and half beer. It is supposed to keep you sober whilst others drink full strength. Well as I was doing the pouring it became 70-30, beer and lemonade. So it was not long before the alcohol began to take effect. It was at that point that Dad figured I was sober enough to drive over to an employee's house over the river on the outskirts of town. Always full of confidence in my ability to do most things, Dad tossed me the keys to carry out the instructed task.

I had just enough blood in my alcoholic system to gun the car into the main street at high speed taking the first bend on the wrong side of the road. Then I hit the straight, across the town bridge, across the Pacific Highway and onto a dirt road that led to the front yard of my intended passenger's house. A large trail of dirt hung in the air for some time, and as it started to clear,I sighted the law in the form of a dust-laden policeman seated on an equally dust-laden motorcycle. Freddy the copper tore strips of me, for everything he had a mind too and warned: "If it wasn't for the fact that you are Eric's son, I would lock you up and throw away the key. Never let me catch you driving like that again." Thankfully there was no breath test in those days as I might well have been over the limit despite the fact that I had been drinking shandies for so many hours. It so happened that Freddy the motorbike copper pull; me over on another occasion for driving erratically along the Pacific Highway, but I quickly talked my way out of it explaining that the steering was defective. He checked it out by feeling the play in the wheel and just said: "You best get this dangerous machine to your Father's workplace right now and get it fixed." With that, he turned his bike around and zoomed off. Once out of sight, I continued on my way to the next town on a personal mission that took precedence over the copper's advice. Whilst I did report the play in the steering to Dad later in the day, I wasn't going to let any copper tell me what to do. Of course, time proved different for me later, but the Police on more than one occasion was on my side, as I related earlier of my drinking sessions with Alex the Russian Engineer, and the Dangerous Dan episode.

My romantic involvements had me soon purchase a column gear Holden in preference to a four-on-the-floor Toyota I then owned. For I always had car cuddles in mind as any hot-blooded racing car driver would do. Just outside town, a kilometre or so past the Police station at the edge of the town boundary was an old dirt airstrip. So, one mad weekend a team of chicken run driving enthusiasts met on the strip and drew straws to see who would race who in a 'Chicken run' to the town boundary.

It so happened that my mate Ash and I won the first ballet. So the idea was that we would first race along the airstrip and do a three-sixty-degree wheel spin at the end of the strip, then gun the cars to the end of the strip, race on the dirt road to a sharp right-hand bend, then a tight left and on to the last kilometre straight stretch to the town boundary. The trouble was we had to cross a single-lane bridge near the end of the race only one car was likely to make it whilst the other, if keeping up neck a neck speed, unless he stopped before the bridge would end up in the 'Deep Creek.' below.. So as it happened Ash and I were neck a neck, side by side until the approach of the bridge. There was no way I would accept being the 'chicken' back then, I would rather die than do that. Ash stopped just short of crossing the bridge and I did my best to slow the vehicle to be within the speed limit as I drove past the Police station. Ash gracefully accepted defeat but none was game to call him "chicken," because none of the others attempted the drive after us.

Ash, as it turned out later married the girl of his dreams and I was his best man. He later joined the Police Force and reached the rank of Sergeant before he tragically died of a heart attack a couple of decades later. He had always proved himself as a superb athlete in professional foot running in his youth, but he was an addicted cigarette smoker and did not quit in time to save his life.

One may be forgiven for saying that I had the 'Coppers' in my pocket when it came to capers in cars that I didn't get booked for. In truth, it was probably the luck of the Irish, my doggedness in protecting my innocence, or maybe the fact that I could sell my way out of anything- well mostly. The first of these get-out-of-jail-free events so happened when I was drinking with a local Sargent of Police in a country town RSL after visiting there for a Rotary meeting. Well in my cups with the cop, we both were the last to vacate the premises after the meeting.

It was a mid-winter night, the fog was low as we ventured outside to the street. The cold air seems to kick in the fuzzy fog in my head duplicating the street scene. I had parked my car nearby, and the off-duty copper was parked nearby too. He hadn't made it back to the Police car before he heard an almighty crash. In my skill to stay on the right side of the road, I made a fatal mistake, one that the rule book says you just don't do. I had turned the wheel abruptly to avoid running over a dog that came running out of the mist in front of me not more than two minutes after I began my inebriated journey home. Whilst I did miss the dog I ran the company car to smack bomb into a tree on what was known as 'The Avenue of Trees.' Well, my quick-to-sober-up drunk drinking partner Copper was quickly on the scene. We left the scene of the crime with the car wrapped neatly around the tree, and he drove me to the Police station for a statement. He put pen to paper and began to ask me questions, about what happened. I said, " I swerved to avoid hitting a dog." My fine feathered friend looked up seriously from the police report of the accident he was writing and said, matter a fact like: "There was no dog." He could see that I was perplexed as to his reply, and having granted me absolution for the crime that wasn't committed by saving the life of man's best friend, he stopped writing, handed me the blank report and said: "Sign here at the bottom of the page, I'll fill out the rest later, you have nothing to worry about." My best friend in blue held the passenger door of the police car open and said: "Don't worry about the damage to your company car either, I'll arrange for it to be towed to the repairer in the morning." I was not exactly welcomed by my then-missus as I arrived home complaining of a headache and went straight to bed. I explained as much of the happenings of the night before that I felt permitted to say to her over breakfast before she drove me off to work. Later in the day, I visited both the police to check out the accident report which read like a CV for a job interview. I was more thankful and content, but even more so when the company car was delivered to my door by my friend the copper with a firm smile: "This one is on the housemate, but it will be your shout after the next Rotary meeting.. Further in the interest of the safety of stray dogs, I will be driving you home at the end of the evening."

The phone rang with much urgency and the voice on the other end spoke matter of fact like: " Doug, this is Sergeant Bruce, just to let you know the local coppers from Armidale will be visiting town on a safety blitz around 9. a.m. So you best tell your customers to be sure they're wearing their seatbelt, otherwise, they will go for a row." It was another drinking mate copper from another time and place and the warning was for me. I was running the local news agency and it was my consistent habit around about nine of clock to toss all the rolled newspapers into the back of my utility and drive like a maniac at breakneck speed along the main street, passing by the Police Station, to deliver the papers to mail room at the back of the Post Office. The mailmen for country properties would deliver my papers and magazines and I would slip them a few quid for their extra effort on my behalf. They were most grateful too, for it supplemented the cost of fuel for their regular country road journeys

As I was driving back along the street, I saluted Petty Sergeant Bruce who was standing out front of the Police Station. He never bothered me when I did my paper deliver to the Post Office ignoring the fact that I never wore my seatbelt. The friendly warning on that day meant I owed him a beer after work, As I never ever put on my seat belt when doing my paper deliveries except on this occasion. I noted as I drove along the main street that a parked police car from Armidale with two burly coppers in dark sunglasses sat there surveying passing cars.

Mostly the coppers in the bush as well as in the city were fairminded. I could usually talk my way around the bookings for speeding fines, protecting that I had an emergency to attend to, or one of the kids had a croup or I just heard the news that some neighbour's cat died. However, there was always the vigilant letter of the law copper who usually came riding a motorcycle on my tail. The first of these was a new breed wonder on a rainy Friday evening back in Sydney. I had been returning from an Insurance appointment and was pulled over in the pouring rain by a young bright shiny badged letter-of-law cop. He insisted I step out of the car in the pouring rain and waltzed me to the back of my vehicle, pointing out that a tail light was blown on my driver's side. He got heavy about it and insisted on seeing my driver's licence. "What's your phone number," he said. " What's your badge number," I replied. "Don't get smart with me." He squawked as I produced my licence. "well I'm going to book you for driving a defective vehicle." He smirked. I asked him what Police station he was appointed to and he just said " North Sydney" as he revved up his bike and departed the scene, leaving me there wet to the bone. I was livered and I headed straight to the North Sydney Police Station. I plonked down the defect notice and fine on the entry desk and filed a verbal complaint to the sympathetic desk jockey. He took the notices and tore them up in front of me. " Forget about it." He says. " He's a new boy on the beat and a bit too keen. I'll write this off for you but you best get that tail light fixed as soon as it stops raining."

Another booking issued by a motorbike copper was well deserved. I was heading at the time to a Friday drinking session at The Rocks. As I crossed the Harbour bridge on the Cahill Expressway I absent-mindedly headed down the road to the tunnel for the eastern suburbs. My reality hit me as I quickly spun the steering wheel and did a one-hundred-and-eighty-degree turn crossing the mid-road ramp in the process to head to Elizabeth Street and on to The Rocks. and my intended destination. As luck would have it, a bike copper appeared from the underground and spotted me mid-turn. He quickly gunned the bike and followed me to the first set of lights in Elizabeth that turned red. I sat in vain hoping that he would let me go. I was breathing a sigh of relief as I just sat there awaiting the change of lights and when they did the copper just followed me to the next set that turned to red. Again, he sat behind me as I gazed back in my review mirror in hope. I cruised through the green light on my way, when suddenly he pulled up next to me. "Pull over." He said and promptly issued me with a ticket. "You thought you were joining to get off Scott free didn't you?" It was a well-deserved fine, and I accepted it gracefully.

CHAPTER 11.

RUNNING TO STAND STILL

I had been down on the docks at the back of The Rocks to collect a boot full of Irish Malt whisky destined for an Irish Catholic renegade priest I knew. It was a gift from Ireland from a boozer mate of his and he asked me if I would do the duty and collect it off the ship for him. Well, he was staying with some mutual friends out near Parramatta and it was a long drive. I figured I would meet up with a drinking mate to fortify myself before taking the journey west on my mission for the man of the cloth. After all, it was Friday arvo, I was near to The Rocks, and it was my usual practice to do a pub crawl there. So after drinking my way around the pub scene, I got behind the wheel fully intending to deliver the whisky. There and about Summer Hill I had decided I best call into a not-so-far-away girlfriend's house for a cuddle before continuing my journey. Well, it wasn't so far up the road that I was taken out by a speeding car on my right. I didn't have a seat belt fastened and got thrown about the cabin of the car with my arm caught up in the spinning steering wheel. The car came to a sudden crunching halt and I sparing into action, running to the now smashed-up offending vehicle. Sticking my head in the driver-side window I enquired of the occupant's state of being. I was informed that one was injured. I thankfully walked to the edge of the road and passed out on the footpath.

The very next morning I awoke in the local Hospital with a Police officer standing by the foot of the bed. " How are you?" He enquired. I didn't let on about the pain in my right arm, as I had unknowingly torn my shoulder cuff as a consequence of the accident. The Copper began to pry me with questions. Then he asks;

" How many drinks had you had earlier in the night? "Well?" I said: " I had at least six beers with a mate at Buckley's, another couple at the Shamrock, and finished with a whisky or three at the Wine-Keller before heading west. "I also told him about the boot full of whisky I had collected for the man of the cloth and enquired about the location of my vehicle. He didn't take any notes in his little black book at this stage of the proceedings and informed me that my car had been towed to a local Burwood Smash Repairer and it was in safe hands. The sympathetic policeman began writing in his little black book when I answered his next question. " And what is your recall as to what happened when the accident occurred.." I sat up a little more and had the nurse prop up the pillow behind my head. Well, as I drove along Summer Hill Road, I came to a set of lights that were green, when I began to pass through but turned yellow before I was halfway. At that point, a car jumped the red light to the right of me and took out my vehicle."

"Hum." The Police said. " We're there any witnesses that can collaborate your version of the events?" I took to my powers of recall: "Well, Just before the accident, I did pass a man on a bike who was close behind me when it all happened." The friendly copper smiled and replied: "You are in luck son, we did interview that cyclist and he confirms your story in his statement." So with that the copper put away his little black book, furnished me the address of the Police Station, and left me being attended to by a pretty nurse.

Early the next morning I was released from the hospital and collected by my drinking companion, John of Polish extract, from the night before. We first headed for the Top Ryde Police Station, for I was concerned about how I could justify my drinking in the pending Insurance claim. The desk sergeant informed me that the officer who had interviewed me in the hospital the previous evening was now off duty. So I explained that I needed to make a statement in my Insurance claim about my sobriety and needed to know what was in the policeman report. The desk Sergeant left me for a time returning with the report. He quickly read the statement I was relieved to hear. It read: "No alcohol." The Lord looks after Saints and drunks crossed my mind.

Satisfied that I could safely write in my motor vehicle claim when it came to the question of drinking. " Refer to Police report Top Ryde Police Station." My good friend took me to the Bur-wood Smash Repairs to check out the vehicle. The front of my car looked like it had been hit by a truck and would take a lot of work to rebuild back to roadworthiness. When it came to the boot I was confused. It had not only been pushed out of shape but it had been flattened too. As I had my arm in a sling, I asked my driving companion, John of Polish extract, to grab a nearby crowbar and force open the boot. Miracles of miracles, the luck of the Irish, not one bottle of that Malt whisky was broken. The mystery of the boot being smashed in came to light when a third party made an Insurance claim against me. Apparently, my car had spun around in the accident and the boot first took out a parked car. Another miracle occurred when I got my car back in what appeared in new condition and the insurance company paid the claim without a hitch.

It was not to be the last of my Insurance claims as a consequence of being under the 'affluence of alcohol.' This time around, I had been living in the inner city near Leichhardt with a couple of English labourers to help share rent. On this particular Friday night, we headed for the local laundromat to wash our clothing.

To fill in time I drove them to the Petersham Inn for a few beers whilst awaiting the next cycle of the washing spin. I considered it safe enough to park my car in the alley beside the pub and we took up three stools at the bar and began shouting each other beers whilst surveying the local drinkers. To the right of my sight, I was awake of nine bikers looking rather dangerously my way. The head of the hoods had his woman resting on his shoulder. She was quite a stunner but I was not impressed with the company she was keeping. I gave her the eye and the once over, and she responded with a knowing smile. Well, I turned away and thought no more about it, as we had to leave to return to the laundromat to dry off our clothing. So we ambled back to my car and hopped in. As I started the motor I had a knock on my window, but could hear what the guy was saying. Stupidly I wound down the window and copped a punch to the mosh, which split my lip in the process. So I tried to get out and face up to the hitter, but try as I might, every time I went to get out of the car I got clobbered with another fist to the face.

Meanwhile, "Tony the Rigger" and "Fast Fist" Mike were in the thick of it. Tony didn't have a prayer, even though he was big and strong, one of the nine attacking bikers gave him a " Liverpool Kiss" and using the force of his skull lifted the front teeth right out of "Tony the Rigger" head. "Fast Fist" Mike was holding his own warding off three of the attackers with wild punches. I am still the bouncing punching bag for the block who won't give me a chance to get out of the driver's seat. And as for the rest of those hoods, they just ripped my car to shreds. Busting the doors of their hinges, using the wiper blades to carve deep scratches across the bonnet.

By this time I managed to make it upright long enough to start the motor, and now angry as a raging bull I cried out to my fighting Poms: " Get in" and I gunned the wreck of a car backwards out of that alley in the hope that would I would kill a few of the bikers in the process. The car came to a screaming halt in the middle of the road and I was out on my feet ready to take on the world in open combat. The local yokels from the pub came giving advice: "It's no use mate" One said: " They have done the damage and left the scene. You are not the first they have done this too. It happens most Friday nights around here. "

 I noted that the beauty had left with beast and I made a mental note never to smile or wink at a biker's mole ever again, and stick to my Friday night drinking haunts in the future. My car was not the worry as I knew another well-written Insurance claim would see my car back on the road without offending the content of my pockets. I was more upset about" Tony the Rigger" losing his teeth as a result of my attraction to the biker mole and having to get five stitches in my upper lip as punishment for my indiscretion.

I was still a creature of habit, though and on another Friday night drinking session, this time with "Stan the Man" and " Dangerous Dan." I had arranged to pick Dangerous Dan up at his new unit location in Lane Cove. So after too many beers in town with Stan the Man, we headed north and turned off the Pacific Highway at Crows Nest westward on River Road towards Lane Cove. It was raining cats and dogs, poor visibility, and I was driving far too fast for the wet conditions. As we rounded a bend in the road heading down a somewhat steep incline, the vehicle began to move sideways down the hill. I was thrown out of the driver's seat and into the arms of my passenger, Stan the man. In his inebriated state he simply responded with" What are you doing over here Zhavigo, you should be driving." I somehow spun the steering righted the car, and was on the way again.

This was almost the last of my drunk driving episodes with Satan the Man and Dangerous Dan, although I can verify a litany of near misses in sobriety sometime later. Incidentally, Stan, the Man had changed my handle from McGuirter, pinned on me by my former first boss in the CTB bank, as a consequence of us both seeing the movie Dr. Zhavigo. In Stan's mind, I had the appearance of Omar Sharif in his role in the film, and as I was dating a rather beautiful English blond, in his mind's eye, she had the appearance of Julie Christie, Zhavigo lover in the film. Whilst I couldn't see the parallels myself, I accepted Stan the man's character evaluation. It was Stan's way of giving me a status by inviting a new nom de Plume for a fair-weather friend he hoped to use for mischievous purposes somehow, sometime in the future. Of course, this never happened as Stan the Man, in league with another character bordering on the edge of the darkness of the wrong side of the law, fell into a dubious occupation not far down the track after that night of drinking.

Stan had already made his bad-boy connections and was heading for even greater downward spiral activities. By the time I caught up with him again after that Friday night drinking spree with him and Dangerous Dan, I was in a full-time relationship, living a 9 to 5 lifestyle, staying out of the limelight and other than my exploits on the grog I had found some semblance of stability. Then I popped the question to the one I thought would be the love of my life. It worked well for a while as I soon recognised that nothing makes woman happier than to see her man overburdened by a heavy mortgage. I spent many years running to stand still, and as fate would have it, she up and left me for another, but that is a story for another time.

Anyhow, back to 'Stan the Man' And his new sidekick in crime 'Mick the Horse Whisperer.' Both of these would be men of wine, women and song ultimately had a problem with the horses. In those days you could borrow money from finance companies without security. However, the interest rate meant these dubious characters could not raise the readiest to meet the required payments. So in their wisdom, or one might say lack of it, they borrowed from another finance company to pay the interest and some of the debt on another, and the cycle continued until the final loan shark insisted on security over the loan before they would release the funds. So in desperation, Stan approached his ageing mother and had her sign over the deeds of the ranch to, the finance company.

Well as any reformed gambler knows, those caught in the trap of compulsion to gain money the easy way just can't stop placing bets on anything that looks like a winner, be that a horse, galloping dog, one-armed bandit, or card game. Stan was hooked and could see no way out of his predicament and for a brief moment he had a vision of his mother being left homeless on the street. This was the point where he was staring into the abyss, and the only way out it seemed was to hold up a bank to get the cash, to at least meet the interest bill on the loan to keep his mother safe and snug as a bug in a rug in her own home. All moral principles went out the window at that moment of realisation that bank robbery was to be his new occupation. Stan had canvassed a branch of the CTB bank the week before. It was one of those out-of-the-way small branches and it entered Stans' troubled mind to devise a plan to rob it. So after showing the game plan to his despairing sidekick, he convinced him that this was the solution to save his mother's home and in the process get them both out of financial bother. Not having an alternative plan 'Mick the Horse whisperer agreed.

Stan no longer owned a car caught a train to Wynyard Station, made his way up to Martin Place and stole a car for the purpose of use during the robbery. Mick was waiting for his return at a duly appointed designated location on the north side of the harbour. They headed up the back streets and through the Lane Cover Park to a nearby little shopping centre. It had a one-of-a-kind CTB bank Branch that could have easily passed for a sub-agency. It was the one Stan had checked out before, he realised it handled a host of local customers who saved more than they spent. He knew from his banking days it would carry a lot of cash for both deposits and weekend withdrawn monies of its customers.

It was five minutes to closing time when the two highway robbers entered the bank's premises. The teller was busy tallying up the final count for the day to balance the books. Likewise, the junior staff member had one of those coin-counting contraptions and was in the background making a lot of noise and shaking the thing. The manager was in his office with his door opened clearly visible behind his desk talking to a customer seated opposite. Mick the Horse Whisperer headed straight for the Manager's Office with Stan the man in hot pursuit, calling out as he jumped the counter: "Drop to the floor, this is a hold-up." Both desperadoes were not well masked. In point of fact handkerchiefs in bandanna style folded above the nose and tied behind the neck in a knot. Stan had nothing more than a tyre lever wrapped in a cloth giving the appearance of a gun. Mick on the other hand was waving a machete he had pinched the day before at a disposal store.

The Manager and chatting customer quickly obeyed the command and hit the deck, as did the teller and junior staff member. Mick watched Stan from the Manager's office door as he unloaded the cash from the tellers box. It was a minute to the closing hour when a little old lady marched in and straight to the teller counter with her passport. She handed it across the counter with a pile of cash and requested to make a deposit. Stan meanwhile had dropped his mask down but still left his sunglasses on.. Stan took the money from the little old lady who seemed half blind anyway. He entered the transaction deposit in her savings account passbook, stamped it with a seal of approval, then as a would-be teller wished her a pleasant afternoon and watched her depart.

It was standard practice for a teller to have a gun under the counter with one bullet in the chamber. In my time in the bank, we were taught to shoot first and ask questions later. Regular pistol practice with the Police being the order of the day, Stan thought it wise to run with the gun and the loot in hand. Mick turned to look for Stan and realising he had already left the premises, gave a last-minute instruction to the Manager and staff to keep their heads down and stay put. Stan had parked the car some 500 meters from the little village centre and Mick covered the distance in world record time. He caught up to Stan as he turned the vehicle around facing the back entry to Lane Cove National Park. They had pulled off a daring delight robbery with nothing but a tyre lever, knife, two handkerchiefs and sunglasses. Stan dropped Mick with the loot at a pre-conceived hiding place and return over the Harbour Bridge, parked the car exactly where he had stolen it from. He had hot-wired it to start it in the first place, so he simply reversed the procedure, attached the wires under the dash, locked the car with its window button on and headed for Wynyard to board the train North. The unsuspecting car owner who had been on a long shopping spree did not even know that her car had been used in a daring daylight bank robbery. The two newly qualified bank thieves returned to making insurance telephone appointment calls at the North Sydney office of the insurance company for the rest of the afternoon.

On the same evening as their robbery, Stan, Mick a mutual friend and I met in the city for a bite to eat before heading off to the movies. Stan had picked a newly released film he thought we would all like to see: "Butch Cassidy and the Sundance Kid" was his choice. I recalled the last scene in the movie as Butch and Sundance were surrounded in a room in a Mexican standoff and about to die, after robbing a nearby Bolivian bank, Butch had convinced Sundance that he had a great idea if they survived this ordeal. " We will go to Australia," said Sundance. "Australia." quirked Sundance: "it's probably just like Bolivia. "No way." replied Butch "The beaches are grand, the women are beautiful and the banks are easy to rob." The dialogue by the about-to-die bank robbers was muffled by Stan and Mick in a roar of laughter. I just didn't think the dialogue was so hilarious. Well at that time I did not know the reasons behind their nervous outburst. I was later informed by Stan the man later over a couple of beers in a nearby pub of their daring bank robbery and how much loot they had acquired as a result. In the following three days, they each deposited cash at different banks and transferred the necessary funds to the finance company for the release hold over Stan's mother's house and they pocket the remainder to gamble at the next day's race meeting.

It was the day after Stan had advised me of the robbery that my conscience got the better of me and I made my way to Miller Street North Sydney in my lunch break to the back lane of the Police Station intent to dob in my long-standing mate so that I could have a clear conscious. Sitting in the gutter at the rear of the Police Station, I realised I could not do it and felt all alone with no friend to share the burden that troubled me. As it happened Peter the Irishman, an agent who was busy recruiting 'candidates' for Scientology in his spare time, sided up to me as I sat contemplating my next move. He enquired as to my state of mind and what was worrying me. Before I had time to answer Peter blurted out: "You not worried about Stan and Mick holding up the Commonwealth Bank are you?" It was a relief to find the two men of guilt conscious had told half the staff in the Insurance office and were that very hour on their way to Cardinal Gilroy at St.Mary's Cathedral to confess their 'sin' to the priest. The Cardinal in his wisdom apparently advised them to give themselves up appealing to the mercy of the courts as first offenders.

I got a phone call from Stan's elder brother who happened to be in Sydney for a conference and he asked me to join him for lunch. We met in the city and he outlined what had happened when the 'men of goodwill' handed themselves into the police and what had taken place when he visited them both in a holding cell at Long Bay jail to await their trial. The circumstances of the need to save the Mother's home, the fact that they were first offenders and their contrition to the judge that they would not 'sin' again stood them in good stead. They were released on a good behaviour bond with the proviso that they repaid the CTB bank thirty dollars per week until their debt was extinguished.

Mick the Horse Whisperer went straight from goal and got counselling for his gambling addiction. However, Stan keeps up the way of life of a criminal. He got himself a job with Chubb Safe learning how the fail-safe locking device works from the inside out thus paving the way for a would-be-safe cracker to make his mark. Then 'Stan the Man' took to holding up banks again and when it became too hot for him in New South Wales he headed to Queensland to pursue even bigger bank jobs for a couple of years. Just ahead of the law, he ended up in Victoria where he made a lucrative living as an underworld bank robber. He was caught in action on a bank job but escaped with a great deal of cash. He apparently believed he was unlikely to be captured. However, the Police had other ideas and were waiting for him at his living quarters in Melbourne.

Stan spent the next twelve years in jail and was advised on release if he crossed an interstate border he would be taken immediately back to prison. I never heard from him again except a whisper from another of my one-time bank colleagues who advise me that he had run into Stan the man in a Melbourne street. He was working for a local charity and attending to the aged and kids in the street. Stan had admitted that he did the occasional bag snatching in the street to keep his hand in. I trust the good in him finally outweighed the bad. That is if he is still alive and kicking. I remember two favourite sayings of his when we worked in banking and insurance; " I used to be conceited but now I am perfect." and the other "Alcohol doesn't affect me affect me, affect me." On both counts the conceit and the alcohol won.

CHAPTER 12.

THE LAST HURRAH

At the end of my first year in the insurance business, I decided to take a break and headed to Europe on a three-month holiday. It meant sailing from Perth to Singapore and catching a charter flight to London. It was the cheap way to travel, so I set out for Perth to commence my journey from there. Perth back then was a slow pace larger version of a country town. I enjoyed my three days in that fair city, frequenting the local bars, drinking different brews, and strolling around, mindful of my fading youth, making the most of the single life with the urging the freedom of leisure being for just a brief time to come. I relished the thought of catching a Russian ship bound for Singapore waiting in Perth Harbour.

It was a small passenger ship with a total of three hundred living souls on board including crew members. A mass of steel from top to bottom. Stepping on board was like entering the Soviet Union. Romantic paintings of lush forests hung at the entry to the stairs as I made my way down two levels on a solid steel staircase along a corridor to my cabin door. It was the one closest to the bow on the starboard side. Like the solid step door entry of alight cabins, the inside was not dissimilar; draped in 1970s-style orange, matching the rest of the hull. No fancy appearance just raw steel coated with some anti-corrosive dull yellowish paint to keep the floating mass safe from the elements of the ocean.

The ship's appearance reminded me of the harsh realism of a Russian capitalist with the zeal for no thrills economic growth of the Motherland versus the soft sweat-smelling fancy artificiality of cruise ships of a Western Democracy's consumerism. It was a time of sex, drugs, rock n' roll and magical free-thinking bliss of what would prove to be more time-wasting and misuse of precious resources. A time of misguided almost novel false beliefs that proved to be ultimately to our Western values' detriment.

Observing the three swinging hammocks and steel welded wall cabinets in my cabin, I noted that the other two bunks already had been tagged by fellow passengers. I duplicated their habit tossing a clothing bag on the hammock and my remaining personal possession next to the only tiny porthole with a screw latch to allow in some air from outside the ship. Making my way back along the corridor of cell accommodation, the sense of a lost silent world entered my spirit, except for the sound of the engine churning, the vessel felt lost in slumber. Listened to The ship's passengers busy in their cabins I cast my fate to the four winds of chance and the Russian crew of almost militant persuasion and made my way up the steel stairs again intent on heading for the bar.

At the top open deck, I opened a heavy steel door and ventured out into the fresh air. I observed a small front timber floored balcony and rail at the bow and steering quarters with an observation deck. Enough room to relax and take in the fresh sea air in calm seas. Towards the bow deck was a sold timber ladder attached to a steel pole mast to the Crow's Nest for distant observation. The Captain's cabin accessible from below deck sat towards the stern. At the stern was a square swimming pool painted blue and left empty. Apparently, the crew filled it up after a couple of days into the journey with fresh seawater. It was once more emptied before entry to the Port of Singapore. An easy way of keeping the pool clean and thus saving on pool chemicals.

I had made my way along three levels of corridors and steel doors above the engine room. The crew of Russians slept on the lower deck near a meeting room stacked with chairs. Nearby a small library with a writing desk and many books on Russia which I also noted were all in English. I flicked through a few of the mainly Russian authors generally known to Western readers. No doubt these had been shipped in to have us believe Russian literature outshone Western taste.

I climbed back up the steel staircase entered the first-level kitchen on the port side and checked out the menu. The meal menu was in Japanese, Russian and English. Kaska porridge, bread, butter and ham sandwich, boiled egg and cottage cheese were the order of the day. A Russian salad was provided with the evening meal as an additional bonus to the daily diet. I later learned that Russian Caviar, a red sturgeon fish was available with every meal and was in plentiful supply. The Russian barmen later advised that the ship was on loan to Fairways for a short-term assignment from Perth to Singapore route and would soon return to its main task of ferrying passengers from Tokyo to Vladivostok to join the Trans Siberian rail link to Moscow, a distance of some 9,258 kilometres. I did come to check it out years later, and the old rusty hull was still holding up on that perilous crossing for the remainder of the 20th century.

As fate would have it the ship was certainly going to have to prove its metal of 'Russian built ' on this voyage to the Orient. I found the bar and made friends with the two young men from Perth I was destined to share my cabin with. We were joined by Aart a Dutch photographer on his way back home to Holland after completing a photo shoot assignment In Western Australia. These three intrepid travellers were to play a vital role in my journey on board and later on in London and Europe. Ian had just finished a contract with the Department of Environmental Planning and his sidekick Peter, a musician was taking long service leave after 5 years of teaching. Aart joined us frequently at the bar when trying to sleep in his cabin proved difficult. Drinking Russian vodka and copious amounts of Russian beer was the order of the day for us intrepid adventurers. Our cabin being not big enough to swing a cat, the bar became our floating home so to speak. In truth, it was our only refuge in the pending cyclonic weather that lay ahead.

We were only a day out to see on our voyage when an initial warning was announced over the intercom by the Captain indicating we were shortly destined for some rough weather ahead. It proved to be a lot worse than the Russian captain had initially indicated. After the evening meal, my newfound friends and I headed for the cabin to unpack our gear, and take a shower before flaking in our hammocks. The ship rocked me to sleep as the ocean waves tilted bow to stern repeatedly throughout the night. In the early hours of the morning, the movement of the ship had changed dramatically. Another announcement by the ship's Captain was a fair warning of the violence of the cruel sea ahead. The message from the Australian Coast Guard had given the coordinates to the Captain to steer a course away from the pending cyclone. Unfortunately, the ship's captain had misunderstood the advice and headed straight ahead towards the centre of a major cyclone. We were already being tossed around the cabin and made our way up to the kitchen. We did our best to hold on to porridge, plate and spoon and get the binding food down the gullet before once more adjourning to the bar. it was the only place on board where we had seats and rails to hold on to as the sea angrily took revenge on the hardy Russian hull.

The next couple of days and nights we spent the time between bar and kitchen, as it was impossible to sleep in the cabin. The ship's bow rose high like a mountain that seemed to take forever to climb. Equally, this action was repeated in reverse as the ship nosed-dived down the steep wave on the other side. We did our best to hold on to the bar and kitchen bench during that violent cyclone. The ship would repeat this process twice straight into the wave and on the third wave, it hit the side of the ship causing it to broadside. The impact of this third wave had the ship shuddering and creaking like it was about to crack wide open. We tolerated this for three days with nothing to do but eat, drink and hold on to whatever kept us upright. Occasionally I headed for the cabin and wedged myself into the hammock catching a short moments of sleep before it got too much and I headed back to the bar.

Early on the fourth morning, Aart the Dutch photographer came up with a bright idea over drinks. He had decided to unlock the main side hatch and attempt to climb to Crows Nest intent on taking a photograph of the ship's bow as it went down the valley of a wave. I had just enough drink in me to develop Dutch courage and I agreed to go with him. We made our weaving way to the large steel door that was securely locked as part of the Captain's instruction to the crew to 'batten down the hatches.' It took all our strength to unwind the wheel lock to that the steel door and make our way outside. Aart and I, with some difficulty against the cyclonic wind and rain, managed to close the fridge like a steel door and wind it locked from the outside. No sooner had we completed this task and the ship began to climb another wave. Hanging on for dear life we were almost washed overboard a number of times as made our way towards the bow, hanging on hand over hand, up the slop of the deck, holding on to the guard rail. Aart had the added burden of his camera in a waterproof case slung around his neck as he led the way with me in hot pursuit. We made it to the main mask and began our steep climb at an angle, like climbing a ladder lying against a wall. Aart was two rungs ahead of me and made it to the Crows Nest, quickly taking his camera from the case to prepare for the downward motion of the ship. At this point, all we could see was the mountainous wave on the rising sea above us. Aart was well prepared and I, stone-cold sober now, hung on to the mask and rail as if my life depended upon it. I was too wet and cold to be scared and just focused on the front of the bow as it made the crest of the wave pausing briefly at the top before heading almost nose-first downward towards the trough below.

It was like riding the big dipper at a fun parlour, but in truth, it was no fun. Holding on for grim death, I watched as the bow of the boat disappeared into the approaching next wave. The nose of the ship to the mast began to vanish in a volume of water and I held on tight taking an almighty impact from the volume of water up the mask. The wave subsided as the ship slowly began to tilt towards the stern. We both made our quick escape down the ladder and on the tilting deck repeated our hand-over-hand return to the steel door. It seemed to take more effort to open the hatch this time but we finally opened it, stepped inside and spun the hatch lock closed just as the ship began to shudder sideways and the third wave hit.

It was a matter of luck that we had made it out on deck when a new sequence of waves began. We had managed purely by luck to start our on-deck ship cyclonic expedition in the right wave sequence, otherwise, we would have been washed overboard on the third wave impact and the sheer volume of water along the ship hull and deck. The journey back to the bar was our best recourse and I downed a whisky followed by a vodka before heading to the showers. Contemplating the goal to climb that mast in the cyclone, as agreed to with Aart, I had to acknowledge to myself that I would never have the courage or foolhardy notion to complete such a task sober.

The little ship hit the eye of the storm on the fourth day and we came into smooth sailing for a day. It was pleasant on the desk and we sunbaked and swam in the pool which had been left three-quarters full from the cyclonic experience. For the first time on the journey, we met many of the passengers who had not left their cabins for the whole four days. In conversation, we were informed that most had suffered seasickness for the majority of the journey. A buffet lunch on a deck supplied by the Russian chef made for new conversations and some sing-a-long. In the evening we were entertained by the ship's crew and danced the night away. I finally crashed into my cabin with my fellow roommates and slept like a baby in the calm sea. Two more days and nights followed before we finally made our way out of the cyclonic conditions and a smooth sea again. We were but a day away from Singapore and longing for terra-firma.

As part of our charter flight package, we were granted a top-notch resort-style hotel in Singapore to stay in. Wing Fat from my old PMG days was now working for Singapore Telecom so I gave him a call on the chance that he would join us for a meal. As it turns out he did the organising but it would prove to be more than just dinner together. I was called to the foyer on my room intercom and Wing Fat answered:. "Come and join me now," he said: "and bring some friends if you like." As the lift door opened to the foyer, I was greeted by Wing Fat with a warm smile surrounded by what I thought were bodyguards. It turned out to be the Chief of the Singapore Police and an entourage of policemen. Wing Fat was still up to his old tricks and called in a Police favour. We three intrepid travellers lost three days in Singapore before boarding our flight to London. It is now a haze of flashes of memory perhaps best forgotten.

Realising I had made no plans for the future, I made my way from the airport with Ian and Peter, joining them in an Earl's Court private accommodation B & B., unloaded my gear and headed for the nearest bar for a beer. It was the typical English dark brew and I started to throw up after the first couple of beers. I ate and drank sparingly for the next twenty-four hours before boarding a ferry across the channel to Amsterdam in Holland. The night journey was the pits as I lay in the passageway between the inner bar and the outer deck on rough crossing hoping someone would kick me overboard and I would depart this mortal coil drowning at sea; relieved of the vomiting and the dreaded cholera diarrhoea. We reached the port at Amsterdam at dawn and as soon as I made it ashore I contacted Aart, the Dutch photographer who had promised us three newfound friends a place to stay on our arrival at Amsterdam. Both Peter and Ian had considered staying in the city at a hostel but agreed to come along with me after Aart had given me directions to his father's home.

We caught a bus to Halfwegg, a medieval little village halfway between Amsterdam and the Hague and followed Aart's directions along the main canal of Harrlemmertrekvaart; the oldest of the canals of Holland. The bridge across the canal with a small Medieval Castle-like walkway was all that the little township had to offer. All I desired was a bed and a room I could call my own. Aart had already left for a photoshoot job on the other side of the country and his Father who spoke limited English reluctantly gave me a room alone. For Peter and Ian, he arranged two beds in another small room. Because of our host's uninviting attitude, they had made up their minds to stay one night only. By the next morning, I was running a fever and bedridden. I had no choice but to stay in bed all the next day. Both my friends were pleased to leave the house and I could see the relief on the Father's face as they hit the road again. Ian promised me he would return as soon as he found a place to stay near Amsterdam and take me with them to share accommodation.

My unpleasant host brought me some chicken broth around mid-day and as I ate he gruffly requested in broken English for me to move on too. My condition had not improved when early the next day Ian returned to let me know he had found an attic flat a little closer to Amsterdam and it had three beds, so we had our digs for the next week. The old Dutchman gave me a friendly handshake, but I gathered by his manner that he was more than glad to rid his home of a sick young man, much less a foreigner. I gladly moved in with my intrepid travellers and upon arrival flaked and slept fitfully for the next twenty-four hours. There were no shower facilities in our accommodation and no toilet nor tap for a drink of water, so we made our way to the Turkish bath about ten minutes up the road. The barman supplied us with clean towels, and use of the pool and bathroom facilities before we returned for refreshments at his bar. I couldn't stomach any food but a small cup of Turkish coffee which sustained me for our bus ride into Amsterdam. I was thankful for the summer heat and left Peter and Ian for their exploration of the city. Nightfall came and I caught up with the boys for a snack at a bar and drug smoke house. Upon entry, I was invited to sit down cross-legged with a group of American hippies whilst they passed around a bong in a large pipe. I took more than my fill each time the pipe was passed to me. I was as high as a kite when I made my way to the bar for a drink; it was like walking on air in slow motion. I felt nothing but peace and a sense that all would be well. I don't recall returning to the attic at our temporary premises, but apparently, I flaked for three days. Peter and Ian had woken me long enough to get some water and bread in my system. They even went to the trouble of purchasing a bed pan and toilet paper in the event that I needed to get up to use the facilities during the night.

I don't recall much at all of those lost days but woke up after what seemed an eternity feeling a bit drained, but over the virus and reenergised to some degree. At the end of the week, we found a youth hostel dormitory facility in Amsterdam. It was a large room of double bunks and was always full of mainly young students from the USA. Nearby was a large oval complex that housed some half a million young drug smokers and heavy drug users. About every half hour an ambulance would go roaring by taking some poor soul to the hospital emergency after having overdosed. Hash in particular was in plentiful supply.

Smokehouses were on every second street corner. At night, it cost a gilder, about 80 cents in today's dollars, to enter a smokehouse, listen to groovy music and smoke until getting high. There were no tables or chairs in the places, just an empty room with piped music and the haze of smokehouse hanging, bodies all around the floor and the occasional little child crying for his now stoned mother lost in oblivion nearby.

I quickly recovered from the after-effect of cholera and the desire to take any more hash. My drinking habits had not subsided and I was still smoking a pack and a half of cigarettes a day, so in that sense I was still an addict. I didn't have to travel far to get a sense of a way of life gone wrong. In the bunk opposite me was a young American student in his last year of a pharmaceutical degree. He had taken a gap year to travel the world but never got much further than Amsterdam or Paris. His daily habit was making chess pieces and a stone chessboard. On completion of his creation, he caught the train to Paris, sold the lot for cash then returned to Amsterdam. His life had become an endless cycle of hash smoking, making another Chess set then running out of cash returning to Paris selling his creation, and returning to Amsterdam to smoke more dope.

I repeatedly made my way to a bar which was always full of gay men drinking, looking to pick up another mark. The men young and old kissed openly in the street and held hands. It was a shock for a true believer in male-to-female relationships being the norm, but I was there for the beer and fascinated by the Avant Garde creative types and their crazy world. Female one-night stands were easy to be had anywhere in Amsterdam, especially among the hippie set. The high-risk factor of contracting a venereal-type disease was always a hazard. Every building along the main canal was a red-light district. Prostitutes hung outside the doors at street level and on balconies above or used large truck mirrors reflecting inside their room for the voyeuristic eye on the street below.

We lived cheaply on Dutch beer, bar snacks and our nightly main meals at the city soup kitchen. It was simply a lineup at a back street eat house to be issued with a bowl and spoon. It cost one guilder (AU 80c) to have the large bowl filled to the brim with thick pea and bean soup and a small quantity of pork on the bone or a pig trotter.

One morning I watched in amazement as a red Mustang entered the main square with three very tall and seemingly fit young Negros stepping out. They moved their way in rhythm along the street and called out to clogged feet: "Do you what to buy some shit man." By then I had my fill of Amsterdam and decided to hit the road again. I sat with Ian and Peter studying a map of the Rhine River villages en route and agreed to meet them in Bacharach two weeks from that day. We had enjoyed our time together but now was time for me to take stock and be content to be with myself in solitude. I looked back and waved a last good-bye to the now-fading figures behind me, tightened the straps on my backpack and settled for a long walk to the German border.

The days that followed tramping my way through Holland and across the border had me averaging 20 kilometres a day with a light load on my back. Most of what I carried was summer clothing for I had left the bulk of my world possessions in storage at the Port of Amsterdam for two months for safekeeping. I carried one change of clothing, a light jacket and the barest of essentials for my survival. It was in the midst of a dry hot summer so I never even had a raincoat. As for food and shelter, I was relying on my remaining savings and the youth hostel system to guide and care if I got into difficulty. I had no real plan at that time for the future. In truth, I was a lost soul having left behind a broken relationship once more back home in Australia. At the time I was but two weeks of the altar and marriage when my bride-to-be's mother tried to put pressure on me to fit her template for living and not my own. My intended bride backed her mother's wishes. I needed this time out to clear my head, take stock and consider my future direction in life. The long walk from Amsterdam to Arnhem took five days of relatively easy walking. It was safe on the road so I tramped on making my way to Bonn.

CHAPTER 13

SENSES AND SENSIBILITY

The first familiar sign that came into view was the Australian
flag in full mask outside the Australian Embassy. I had made
it my policy to collect Embassy stamps in my passport. As it
turns out later, the Dutch Embassy stamp proved a blessing
when I finally returned to the Netherlands some two months
later to collect my stored luggage. The Ambassador of Australia of the Department of Foreign Affairs invited me into his
Embassy office of polished mahogany timber desk, chair and
charred timber wall panels. The fittings likewise reeked of
leftovers from the Nazi regime possibly stolen from some
Jewish nobleman during WW 11. He invited me to sit in the
chair opposite and began to ply me with questions about
home. He informed me the newspapers from Australia were
usually a week or two behind current events by the time they
received them and was interested in a layman's view of the
political goings on in Canberra.

The only news I had was that William McMahon replaced
John Gordon as Prime Minister in a 33:33 ballot on a motion
of no confidence in John Gorton as Prime Minister. A gallant
John Gorton, as chairman, gave his casting vote against the
motion, effectively voting himself out of office. He stood for
and won the Deputy Party leader role. We discussed Liberal
politics and the rise of the soon-to-be Prime Minister Gough
Whitlam in the Labor Party. The Ambassador as to be ex-
pected of a high-ranking public servant was a keen cricket
fan. Although I wasn't, he was keen to get my opinion on the
potential of the idea of one-day cricket, the first of which was

a one-day exhibition match between Australia and England in January. The test match had been called off due to extremely wet weather in Melbourne and an exhibition was held to appease the fans and recover some of the MCG financial loss as a result. After much discussion on Cricket, we turned to Rugby Union which I had played for over a decade and followed with passion. I left the Embassy with an Australian Embassy stamp in my passport and a small Australian flag which I later sowed on my backpack to show the world this long-haired and bearded hippie lout was a proud Australian.

I tramped the day away and flagged a lift to the outskirts of Cologne late afternoon. After checking in at a local information centre for the cheapest place to stay, I headed for a youth hostel a few kilometres along the Rhine riverfront and bedded down for a week to tour the city. It had been a training camp site for Hitler youth during the war and was now run by a graduate of those times. The blue-eyed blond man of Arian race greeted me like a new recruit and I was ushered to my room. I stayed there for a few days, checking out all the tourist haunts. On my last day in Cologne, I made my way to the cathedral in a pensive mood. It was at the back of the cathedral, gazing into the ebbing flow of the Rhine River, that I hatched a plan for my future life. I assumed with great confidence that would set me on the road to corporate success and later many more successes in my own business. As it happened it all proved to be true.

So on my return to Australia, I settled into marriage after only one year from sowing my wild oats in Europe. I slowly but surely drifted away from my old haunts as a 'Writer on the Rocks,' but did manage to escape the home life from time to time to go on a drinking spree with other wayward drinking companions. I suffered the wrath of a nagging wife for days after each drinking spree, because I always promised I wouldn't go astray again, but for many years until sanity prevailed I continued terrible drinking habits. The drink seemed to soothe the savage beast that raged within and at the time it all seemed normal. On the surface, if glanced at by an outside observer, all seemed right with the world and our family. It was not so, as I had buried my innermost feelings with alcoholic beverages which for a time quelled the real me.

Measured by the standards of society we had all the trimmings of a perfectly happy, affluent and stable family unit. The crack in my armour began to show as I reached out more and more for external proof of my worthiness. The measurement measure was money, the egocentricity was the actions of what on the surface was for all intent and purpose a benefit to both my family materially and my customer base with the provision of personal service. I can not recall if I was ever happy in my past life as discontent drove me even more in my efforts to fulfil ill-conceived goals. Fate would have it that my time was up and whilst I was at the top of my pathway of apparent success, the downward spiral was just around the corner.

Sure there were some fun times to be had that I now recall in those early years, especially in our days of wine and roses in the bush. Whilst my obsession with work continued I found a new freedom in the company of fellow heavy drinkers both the farmers and graziers and successful business colleagues. Overnight stays on friend properties, resort holidays, and weekend-sporting events for the kids. It seemed all good fun, and we had plenty of laughs that I could go on with here, but the serious side of my drinking was already taking its toll.

At the start of this book, I indicated that the stories within were more about what happened in a comical way before I gave up the booze. However, It would not be fair not to give you the reader an insight into what changed and what it is like now, looking back on my life as it changed to sobriety with the help of the steps of Alcoholics Anonymous.

Sure, there were many happy years, or so it seems now, for a family of drinkers. The mother of my children, and my three sons, before they had even left secondary education, were led to the booze by their parent's drinking habits, home parties with a so-called elite group of friends who ultimately proved fair weather ones, and the circle of private school friend they mixed with at school and beyond. My daughter who came along ten years after my youngest son was much more astute than the rest of the family. She never touched alcohol in spite of having it all around her. To her credit, as soon as she was old enough, she moved on with a final statement: " I have to get away from this toxic family." She went on to pave her own career path in medicine and was accredited with the University Medal for Nuclear Science before branching out into a medical career and marriage to a professional business type. As for the rest of us, well we all battled with the gene of practising alcoholics.

I was riding the crest of the wave of success having made it to the top of the heap in the corporate world of Insurance and finance. Then I branched out after a decade to run my own retail stationary warehouse and an Australia-wide Paper Merchant business. At best I employed forty casuals, providing material affluence for my wife and family, and gave my children the best of private school education, but it wasn't enough. It was not that I didn't care, I did. As the saying goes, there is none so blind as those who cannot see. I was running hard to stand still, caught up in the obsession of being a workaholic and increasingly habitual daily drinker.

Ultimately it got too much for the mother of my children and she left me for another. As I watched all that I perceived as being what I was about crumbling, I began using alcohol as a bandaid to relieve the pain and suffering that I perceived as being a result of the family breakdown. It took a number of years to stop drinking altogether and to realise that what I had lost was not just my family, business and material possessions, but the essence of who I really was within.

It took another decade of drinking with not many fun moments to speak of before I quit altogether. The fellowship of Alcoholics Anonymous and the spiritual programme that followed have helped me stay on the straight and narrow path as a sober alcoholic for nearly two decades now. Whilst I have almost lived a single life again for as long as I did a married one, I am much happier now for I am no longer the person I once was when I was a drinker. The friendships I have within the fellowship of AA and beyond have me conscious of what is important to others. I no longer feel lonely, lost and dejected. Rather I wake clear-headed every morning, keep relatively fit for my age, and am grateful that despite my years of heavy drinking and smoking I have relatively good health and a good life -thanks be to God.

Whilst you may find some of my stories of pub crawls in and around The Rocks, career moves, and travels in my youth, amusing at the very least, I decided to cease telling more of my drinking stories. It's enough to say I've moved on from the ways of my past, those friends and foes I dance a devil may care wasted time with.

Far away from the Rocks of my youth, now, I still have the recall but not the desire to repeat the things of youth in my wild woolly ways. Although I do walk through the crowded streets of The Rocks from time to time, viewing the changes that have taken place there. It's a tourist hub now attracting those who seek to get a glimpse of what once was, but those who visit can no longer see the many old pubs and haunts of the Rocks Push that once existed, now replaced by commercial high-rise Sad but true the drinking class and haunts of yesteryear are a lost cause and just a memory in the minds of those like me who still have a recall of those dandy days of the 1960s.

About the Author.

Doug McPhillips, poet, singer, songwriter, and author, commenced his journey of discovery over a decade ago after life-changing experiences.
The many tracks he has traversed throughout the Northern Hemisphere and down under in New Zealand and Australia have resulted in the facts and fiction of this novel.

Doug has recorded and sung songs interrelated to this work with majestic melody in a true Australian style.
Doug has written several novels, a book of poems, a travel guide and three albums of songs inspired by his travels.

www.caminoway.com.au

Doug is an adventurer who divides his time between creative pursuits, family and friends, and those who may benefit most from his efforts and experience.

AFTERTHOUGHT:

A man came to the AA meeting drunk, interrupted the speakers, stood up and took his shirt off, staggered loudly back and forth for coffee, demanded to talk, and eventually called the group's secretary an unquotable name and walked out. I was glad he was there, for once again I saw what I had been like. But I also saw who I still am, and what I still could be. I don't have to be drunk to want to be the exception and centre of attention. I have often felt abused and responded abusively when I was simply being treated as a garden variety human being. The more I realised that he insisted he was different, the more I realised that he and I were exactly alike.

Oct 5/23

www.ingramcontent.com/pod-product-compliance
Lightning Source LLC
Chambersburg PA
CBHW082058090726
47909CB00011B/3082